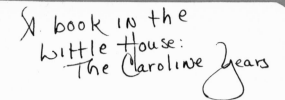
A book in the Little House: The Caroline Years

DATE DUE

DE2 4'98			
AP1 5'99			
JE2 9'99			
AU 2 6 '99			
SE 21'00			
2-15-01			
FE 14 01			
12-2-02			
JE 12 '04			
OC 2 6			
MY 1 3 '1			

F
J   Wilkes, Maria D.
       Little clearing in the
       woods

**Filed on shelf under
'Wilder, Laura Ingalls"**

#3

DEMCO

Little Clearing
in the Woods

The LAURA *Years*
By Laura Ingalls Wilder
Illustrated by Garth Williams

LITTLE HOUSE IN THE BIG WOODS
LITTLE HOUSE ON THE PRAIRIE
FARMER BOY
ON THE BANKS OF PLUM CREEK
BY THE SHORES OF SILVER LAKE
THE LONG WINTER
LITTLE TOWN ON THE PRAIRIE
THESE HAPPY GOLDEN YEARS
THE FIRST FOUR YEARS

The ROSE *Years*
By Roger Lea MacBride
Illustrated by Dan Andreasen & David Gilleece

LITTLE HOUSE ON ROCKY RIDGE
LITTLE FARM IN THE OZARKS
IN THE LAND OF THE BIG RED APPLE
ON THE OTHER SIDE OF THE HILL
LITTLE TOWN IN THE OZARKS
NEW DAWN ON ROCKY RIDGE

The CAROLINE *Years*
By Maria D. Wilkes
Illustrated by Dan Andreasen

LITTLE HOUSE IN BROOKFIELD
LITTLE TOWN AT THE CROSSROADS
LITTLE CLEARING IN THE WOODS

Little Clearing
in the Woods

Maria D. Wilkes

Illustrations by Dan Andreasen

HarperCollins*Publishers*

To my daughter Grace,
who rushed into my life as God's tiniest angel
and keeps me believing in miracles

HarperCollins®, 🏠®, Little House®, and The Caroline Years™
are trademarks of HarperCollins Publishers Inc.

Little Clearing in the Woods
Text copyright © 1998 by HarperCollins Publishers Inc.
Illustrations © 1998 by Dan Andreasen
Printed in the United States of America. For information address
HarperCollins Children's Books, a division of HarperCollins Publishers,
10 East 53rd Street, New York, NY 10022.
http://www.harperchildrens.com
Library of Congress Cataloging-in-Publication Data
Wilkes, Maria D.
    Little clearing in the woods / Maria D. Wilkes ; illustrations by Dan
Andreasen.
        p.   cm.
    Summary: Young Caroline Quiner, who would grow up to be Laura
Ingalls Wilder's mother, and her family move to a new farm near
Concord, Wisconsin.
    ISBN 0-06-026997-9. — ISBN 0-06-026998-7 (lib. bdg.)
    ISBN 0-06-440652-0 (pbk.)
    1. Ingalls, Caroline Lake Quiner—Juvenile fiction. [1. Ingalls,
Caroline Lake Quiner—Fiction. 2. Wilder, Laura Ingalls, 1867–1957—
Family—Fiction. 3. Frontier and pioneer life—Wisconsin—Fiction.
4. Family life—Wisconsin—Fiction. 5. Wisconsin—Fiction.]
I. Andreasen, Dan, ill. II. Title.
PZ7.W648389Lf   1998   97-44602
[Fic]—dc21   CIP
                                                                  AC
Typography by Alicia Mikles
1   2   3   4   5   6   7   8   9   10
❖
First Edition

Author's Note

Before Laura Ingalls Wilder ever penned the Little House books, she wrote to her aunt Martha Quiner Carpenter, asking her to "tell the story of those days" when she and Laura's mother, Caroline, were growing up in Brookfield, Wisconsin. Aunt Martha sent Laura a series of letters that were filled with family reminiscences and vividly described the Quiners' life back in the 1800s. These letters have served as the basis for LITTLE HOUSE IN BROOKFIELD, LITTLE TOWN AT THE CROSSROADS, *and* LITTLE CLEARING IN THE WOODS, *the first three books in a series of stories about Caroline Quiner, who married Charles Ingalls and became Laura's beloved Ma.*

The Caroline Quiner Ingalls whom I've come to know through Aunt Martha's letters, personal accounts, and my own research is, I was surprised and delighted to discover, even more animated, engaging, and outspoken than the fictional Caroline whom millions of readers have grown to know and love. I have presented the most realistic account possible of Caroline Quiner's life in LITTLE CLEARING IN THE WOODS, *while still remaining true to the familiar depiction of Ma in the Little House books. I would like to thank everyone who contributed historical and biographical information and who directed me toward significant original sources, diaries, and documents, especially William Anderson, Martin Perkins, John Janzow, William F. Jannke III, Cindy Arbiture, and Professor Rodney O. Davis.*

—M.D.W.

Contents

Little Clearing
in the Woods

Good-byes

"I forgot to tell Henry to take my chickens!" Caroline exclaimed. Waiting to climb into Uncle Elisha's wagon with her sisters, Martha and Eliza, she suddenly remembered her hens and whirled around to look for her brother.

"Leave Henry alone," Martha said in her most grown-up ten-year-old voice. "He's busy helping Joseph. And Charlie." Smiling happily, she tied her bonnet strings beneath her chin and glanced quickly at the dark-haired boy helping her brothers. "Just think, we'll have two whole weeks with Charlie!" she whispered gleefully.

"I know they're busy," Caroline answered. Looking past Uncle Elisha and the team of oxen he was hitching to his wagon, she watched the flurry of activity taking place in front of the frame house. Her brothers, Joseph and Henry, and their neighbors, Benjamin Carpenter and his son, Charlie, were loading the Quiners' belongings into Mr. Carpenter's wagon. "But what if Henry forgets the hens?" Caroline asked.

"Mother told us to wait by Uncle Elisha's wagon until she comes outside," six-year-old Eliza said primly. Tucking her corncob doll inside her woolen shawl, she added, "She said not to bother the boys and Mr. Carpenter, or else."

Ignoring her little sister, Caroline set her schoolbooks and her rag doll, Abigail, beside a wagon wheel, then dashed the short distance across the cold, dewy grass to Mr. Carpenter's wagon. "Henry," she cried out breathlessly, "don't forget the hens!"

Good-byes

"Every one of them squawkers is packed already," Henry called out as he swung a hay-filled mattress over the side of Mr. Carpenter's wagon into his older brother's waiting arms. "In case you're wondering, Caroline, I brought the rooster along, too. Any empty space left up there, Joseph?"

Joseph surveyed the sacks, barrels, tables, and trunks piled in front of him. Two reed hampers, tightly packed with clothes, were tucked between Mother's butter churn and the three large barrels that held salt pork, flour, and corn meal. A washtub rested in the center of the wagon, cradling a collection of iron kettles and the leftover beans, peas, and potatoes from last fall's harvest. Beside the tub, four wooden chairs rested upside down on top of a square oak table. "A corner here," Joseph told Henry. "And there's some room on top of these chairs, too. What's left?"

"One crate and a small sack of flour," Henry answered, wiping his sweaty forehead with the back of his arm. "And the stove, of course."

"You didn't pile anything on the hens, did you?" Caroline asked as she stepped up beside Henry and peered inside the wagon. "They won't like it one bit."

"If you think I want to find a gunny sack full of dead chickens when we get to Concord, you're mighty mistaken, little Brownbraid," Henry said, rolling his eyes. "Those chickens will be the only food we'll have to eat for weeks!"

"Don't say that!" Caroline cried. Ever since she was four years old, she had cared for the family's hens, collecting their eggs each morning, feeding them, and cleaning out their henhouse. Each year she had even named every one of the birds, and although she knew they weren't pets, she still hated to think about eating them. "And don't call me little Brownbraid, Henry! I'm not little anymore!"

"Eight years old doesn't make you a grownup," Henry teased. "You have to wait till you're twelve, like me! Now get back to Uncle Elisha's wagon, Caroline. We're 'bout ready to go." With a teasing tug at the bottom of his sister's long brown braid, Henry dashed back into the frame house.

"If I was a grown-up, I'd never go away." Caroline sighed as she trudged back toward the wagon.

Six months ago, in the midst of the fall harvest, the Quiners had learned they'd have to leave their home in Brookfield, Wisconsin. The man who owned their homestead had given it to his sister, and Mother needed to find a new place to live. A shiver darted through Caroline as she recalled Mother's reading the awful letter from Michael Woods that told them they'd have to move. It still didn't make sense to her that the little frame house she had lived in all her life could be his, when her father had built it, board by board.

In the first cold days of February, Mother and Uncle Elisha had traveled thirty miles west across a barren, frozen landscape to a little town named Concord. There Mother had purchased forty acres of land. Once the sweet sap began flowing from the maples, Mother had stopped the sewing and mending that kept her busy in the evenings and begun packing the family's belongings. Three weeks later, Uncle Elisha had arrived from Milwaukee in his empty wagon. Friends and neighbors in Brookfield had visited the frame house to say good-bye. Last night, Caroline had said her saddest farewell to her best friend, Anna.

A brisk April wind blew through Caroline's coat and brown woolen dress. She looked one more time past the garden and barn to the farthest corners of their land, where the pale-green marshes were spotted with yellow blossoms. Caroline was tempted to gather one last bouquet of the marsh marigolds, but she knew there wasn't time. So she checked off in her mind each of the favorite places she had visited: the barn, the henhouse, the garden, the old oak tree that tapped her bedroom window as she fell asleep on windy nights. Earlier this morning, Caroline had been in such a hurry, she'd hardly had a moment to feel sad when she said good-bye to each of these places. Now, as she gathered her books and rag doll into her arms, her throat suddenly felt tight.

"You almost didn't get back in time," Martha chided Caroline as they climbed into Uncle Elisha's wagon and sat down on a narrow plank of wood that was securely fastened across the center.

"Henry has the hens, and I finished all my good-byes," Caroline replied, shifting from side to side until she was comfortable. "I have Abigail. I have my books." She felt the bottom of her braid for her green ribbon, then fingered the inside of her pocket for the red plaid one. "My two bows are here, too. That's everything, I think."

Just as Caroline finished speaking, Mother left the frame house and shut the door. "The sweeping's done, and that's the last of it," she called out as she hurried toward Uncle Elisha's wagon with a broom in one hand. Three-year-old Thomas scurried along beside her, carrying a small bundle. "We're ready to leave now, Elisha, as soon as the stove is secure in one of the wagons," Mother told her brother-in-law.

"Carpenter's wagon is full already, Charlotte,

and that stove sure is big. And heavy," Uncle Elisha grumbled.

"I'll give up my seat and walk all the way to Concord 'fore I'll leave that stove!" Mother said firmly. "Henry carried it all the way to Brookfield from Milwaukee years ago, Elisha, so I wouldn't have to cook in the hearth. I certainly don't intend to leave it behind now!"

"I'll go tell Carpenter we need to find room for the stove," Uncle Elisha said soothingly. "Forgive me, Charlotte. I had no idea you were so attached to the thing."

Caroline watched as her uncle hurried to the other wagon and spoke to Mr. Carpenter. Mother turned her attention to her youngest child. "May I have the package now?" she asked.

"I didn't drop it," Thomas said proudly, handing Mother the wrapped bundle he had carried all the way from the house.

"Please hold this for a minute, Caroline," Mother requested, placing the slender package in Caroline's hands. She slid the broom beneath the girls' seat, settled Thomas on the bench in front of them, and turned to look at the frame house one last time.

"What's in there?" Eliza quietly whispered into Caroline's ear.

Caroline ran her fingertips over the bumps and curves beneath the linen wrap. "It's Father's candlesticks," she answered. "They're more precious to Mother than anything."

"We have everything packed now," Joseph said as he approached the wagon. "Even the stove, Mother."

"Let's be on our way then," Mother said, a sudden glint appearing in her weary green eyes. "I haven't set out on such an adventure, Joseph, since you were knee high to a caterpillar!"

"We ride in the wagon to a new house!" Thomas cried out exuberantly.

Uncle Elisha helped Mother onto the bench beside Thomas. "I'm afraid it's just a cabin, Thomas," he said. "But with your mother's flair and sense of style, I've no doubt it'll look finer than a castle come summertime."

"Why, thank you, Elisha." Mother laughed.

"But I think that would take a lifetime to accomplish!" Turning around in her seat, she smiled at Caroline. "I'll take that package now," she said. Caroline handed it back carefully.

"Into the wagon, Henry and Charlie, and we'll pull foot!" Mr. Carpenter's bright voice sailed above the blackbirds' morning song. "There's a wagonload of work awaiting us at the end of the trail!"

"Wolf!" Caroline cried out suddenly. "We forgot Wolf!"

"He can walk along with me," Joseph said, whistling the gray-and-black dog over to his side. "Henry and I will switch places once we've gone a ways."

"I'll walk some, too," Charlie offered, shaking his black hair out of his eyes.

"Suit yourself," Henry hollered. Leap-frogging over Charlie onto the back of the wagon, he stepped over a bench and a basket, and quickly found a barrel to lean against.

The moment Charlie climbed up beside his father, Mr. Carpenter tugged at the reins and directed his team to stop beside Uncle Elisha's wagon.

"You're certain you have everything now, Charlotte?" he asked.

"I've left a few unhappy memories, but I intended to do that," Mother said. Listening from behind, Caroline knew that Mother was thinking about the dark days after they had learned that Father had been lost at sea and was never coming back.

"Just so long as you take the good ones with you," Mr. Carpenter said.

"You're certain Sarah doesn't mind us borrowing you for a few weeks, Benjamin?"

"She wouldn't have it any other way," Mr. Carpenter answered. "I told you, Charlotte, Sarah's gone home to Waukesha to nurse her mother, and she'll stay there till Charlie and I return. That's likely to be harvesttime at our current pace," he joked. "Now let's be on our way, or I'll change my mind and build you a house out back of ours, no matter how much you complain about it!"

Uncle Elisha laughed. "Charlotte refused

to come to Milwaukee to live with us. I've no doubt she'd turn down your offer, too." Pushing his black hat back to the edge of his hairline, he climbed in beside Mother and Thomas and lifted the yoke and chain.

"Sit close to each other, now, girls," Mother said over her shoulder. "The road promises to be bumpy ahead."

"Move out now, fellas!" Uncle Elisha shouted. The wagon pitched forward. Bracing herself against Eliza, Caroline glanced back one last time.

The frame house, the barn, the old oak, and leafy maples grew smaller and smaller as the wagons rattled along. In just a few minutes, Caroline could no longer see the only home she had ever known.

Walking Trees

"Ouch!" Caroline cried as Eliza's head banged into her shoulder. Gripping the side of the wagon tightly, she struggled to stay on the seat as Uncle Elisha's wagon lurched to one side and sharply stopped.

"I can't help it!" Eliza complained. "I wish we could get off this wagon right now!"

"I wish we could go back home," Caroline said under her breath.

Martha leaned across Eliza and pinched Caroline's arm. "Don't be such a fusspot," she scolded. "Mother said the new land is very nice. Besides, Mr. Ben and Charlie would never just up and leave us in some awful place, and Uncle Elisha wouldn't either. We'll be settled in the cabin before they go away. They promised, and I believe them." Turning to her youngest sister, Martha said, "Sit as close to me as you can, Eliza, so the wagon won't toss you around so much. Uncle Elisha says it's at least three days to Concord. No sense complaining when we've barely made it through one day."

Caroline stared ahead silently. Watching wisps of her hair skip about her forehead in the wind, she wondered when her older sister had become so grown-up. Caroline knew Martha was right, but she wouldn't dare admit it. In fact, even though her heart was heavy with thoughts of Brookfield, sometimes she could hardly wait to see the new place she'd soon call home.

"Easy now, fellas," Uncle Elisha urged the oxen. "Move on ahead before you tip the wagon and leave us in one fine fix!"

With a jolt the oxen righted the wagon and

trudged ahead down the bumpy dirt road. The three girls held on tightly to their wooden plank, bouncing and bumping into each other with every hole, hill, and water pool that the wheels rolled over.

"Darned if we shouldn't have moved in the dead of winter, Charlotte, when we went to buy the land," Uncle Elisha said. "Two months ago, the ice made this road much easier to pass."

"But for the cold, Elisha, I'd agree," Mother said. "Had Michael Woods's family not planned to arrive in Brookfield by week's end, I'd have preferred to wait another month to make this journey. The ground wouldn't be so muddy."

"We're traveling to forty acres of wilderness with nothing on it but heavy timber and a log cabin," Uncle Elisha answered Mother. "It's best that we get there soon as we can. We could start clearing trees tomorrow and still not have enough time to turn over a small section of soil for planting mid May."

"Nevertheless, drier earth would have been a far preferable travel companion," Mother insisted, her firm voice shaking with each bump and tilt of the wagon. "And this breeze is likely to have all of us chilled through by nightfall!"

Bowing her head away from the whipping wind, Caroline reached deep into her coat pockets and squeezed the two potatoes that had kept her hands warm since they had left Brookfield early that morning. "My potatoes are as cold as I am," she murmured to her sisters, and tucked her hands beneath the heavy quilt covering their legs.

"Mine too," Martha said. "The trees are walking much faster now than when we left this morning. The faster they walk, the colder it gets, I think."

Thomas clapped and bounced on the seat where he sat huddled between Mother and Uncle Elisha. "The trees are walking!" he cried.

"Trees don't walk, silly," Eliza loudly informed her little brother. "Do they, Caroline?" she asked softly so Thomas couldn't hear.

"None that I ever saw," Caroline said. Shifting restlessly, she peered past Uncle Elisha and the black-rimmed hat that was slanted on top of his head. The wagon rumbled toward a thin blue band of sky that grew wider as it dropped to the horizon, and was surrounded by sprawling branches and budding leaves. As the wagon moved forward down the corridor of trees, Caroline suddenly thought the trees *were* moving while the wagon stayed in its place. She blinked hard, and when she opened her eyes, the trees again stood still as the wagon jolted past them.

"We're not far from the homestead where I hope to spend the night," Uncle Elisha told Mother. He leaned forward and scanned the horizon. "Do you remember Joe Albert, Charlotte?"

"The same Joe Albert who grew up with you and Henry in New Haven?" Mother asked.

Hearing Mother mention Father's name, Caroline listened closely. She hoped Uncle Elisha would have a good story to tell.

"One and the same." Uncle Elisha nodded. As if he sensed Caroline's eyes on his back, he raised his voice a little. "Wasn't for Henry,

Joe would have drowned before he ever saw his tenth birthday. He and Henry were fooling on a thin patch of ice one winter morning when we were boys. The ice cracked, and Joe fell through. Henry soaked himself to the skin pulling his friend out of the freezing water, and Father caned him good when he arrived home covered in ice and snow and hacking like a donkey. Joe never forgot that Henry saved his life. Even after we all headed west, Joe sent an occasional letter to Henry or me. Latest word 'fore I left was his wife had delivered their first child—Sarah Anne, I think they named her. I sent Joe a letter telling him I'd be moving Henry's family to Concord come spring, and we'd be traveling the road that passes his homestead. He kindly offered us two rooms in his house, and the extra space in his stable to sleep in."

"I'll be indebted to him for his kindness," Mother said. "I thought we'd spend the night in the wagons."

"I expect we'll be nearing his house by candlelight," Uncle Elisha said. "It's down a ways beyond the next clearing, if I'm not mistaken."

The thought of a warm place to sleep cheered Caroline, and she grew even more excited when the dense forest thinned into a tree-lined meadow fringed with tall grasses that tilted to and fro in the wind.

Uncle Elisha pulled steadily on the yoke and chain, and called, "How, fellas!" Obediently, the oxen turned off the road and moved slowly southward. The wagon tipped and shifted as its wheels rolled through the soft ground still moist from melted snow and early spring showers.

We'll stop soon now, Caroline thought. She gripped the side of the wagon tightly and looked back for Mr. Carpenter's wagon. The sun dipped below the darkening border of sky and earth, bathing the meadow in a soft blue-and-gold light. Daylight was fading, but Caroline could still see her neighbor's friendly wave, and she waved back. Henry was riding in the wagon beside Mr. Carpenter, his sandy curls blowing behind him, his lips pursed in a whistle. Joseph and Charlie walked along beside the wagon, Wolf keeping stride between them.

"Is Carpenter still following us?" Uncle Elisha called out from the front of the wagon. "It just occurred to me that he has no idea how to get to Joe's homestead."

Caroline was about to shout, "Yes, sir," when a series of shrieks and whinnies suddenly screeched through the air. Caroline whirled around again and watched in horror as Mr. Carpenter's wagon tilted sharply and tottered in the air on two wheels. Holding tightly to the reins, Mr. Carpenter frantically slid to the other side of the wagon beside Henry, but it was too late. The wheels touching the ground collapsed beneath their weight, and the wagon crashed over on its side, tossing out Mr. Carpenter, Henry, and most of the Quiners' belongings. One of the black horses fell with the wagon and lay kicking its bony legs furiously in the air. The other stamped the earth, the wagon wheels behind it still spinning high above the ground.

"Stop!" Caroline shouted.

"Whoa!" Uncle Elisha commanded his team, and he leaped off the wagon as the wheels rolled to a halt.

"Stay in the wagon, Thomas. Eliza, hold these candlesticks, and don't lose sight of them," Mother directed, handing Eliza her precious bundle. "Martha, Caroline, come with me."

Mother helped Caroline and Martha down from their seats, and they ran to Mr. Carpenter's wagon.

"Dash it all!" Mr. Carpenter was shouting as they hurried to his side. Scrambling to his feet, he banged his fist against the back of the wagon. His usually calm face was twisted with anger, and his dark eyes were furious. "What possessed you to take us off the road like that, Quiner?"

"I was leading the wagons to the homestead I told you about!" Uncle Elisha cried defensively.

"You never mentioned that this homestead was so far off the territorial road," Mr.

Carpenter bellowed. Without another word, he pulled the horse on the ground to its feet and unbridled the team, patted their heaving sides, and calmed them down. Then he confronted Uncle Elisha again, his tone surly. "Had your friend lived on the road or even down a beaten path, it was the right thing to do. Turning into this meadow was asking for trouble! It's fixed us good."

Caroline had never seen Mr. Carpenter look so angry. She stood silently, staring up at him in disbelief.

"I was as surprised as you that Joe lived so far off the road," Uncle Elisha admitted. "Still, there's no sense getting yourself in a pucker now that the damage is done. Let's set the wagon upright and get it loaded again."

"I'm afraid Henry may be hurt." Mother's voice stopped the two men in their tracks and quenched their heated words instantly.

Caroline dashed around to the other side of the wagon with Martha and Mother. Joseph and Charlie were kneeling beside Henry, who was sprawled on his back, cradling Mother's

22

mahogany clock in his arms. Crates and barrels, bulging sacks, and a bundle of quilts tied with heavy twine had been tossed to the ground along with him. A large settle lay beside a wooden trunk at his feet.

"Are you all right, Henry-O?" Mother knelt down and gently stroked his brow. "Does anything feel broken?"

"I was just telling Joseph, no bones broke here. Got the wind knocked out of me, is all." Henry sat up quickly. "I saved the clock," he added with a grin.

"Thank you." Mother smiled gratefully, taking the instrument out of his hands. "Now sit still for a moment, please."

"Are you hurt?" Martha asked Joseph and Charlie. "Your clothes are all dirty."

"That's what we get for diving out of a falling wagon's way," Charlie said, trying to wipe the mud off his face. "I'm going to take the horses from Pa and put them on a picket line to quiet them some. Holler if you need me."

"I'll come along with you, and see to Eliza and Thomas," Martha quickly decided.

Joseph stood up and rubbed his sore shoulder. "We were walking alongside the wagon, Mother, and saw the front wheel sink into the ground. The back dipped, and *wham!*" He clapped his hands together hard. "Me and Charlie barely got out of the way before the whole thing tipped. Henry and Mr. Ben got the worst of it."

"This wheel's got the worst of it," Mr. Carpenter called out from the other side of the wagon. "It's cracked but good and will need fixing before it can handle such a heavy load again."

"I'll take it to my friend," Uncle Elisha offered. "Charlotte and the girls can come along with me and stay the night in his house. Joe and I will fix the wheel, and I'll have us all back on the road at daybreak."

"We should stay together, Elisha," Mother advised, "no matter where we sleep."

Standing up, Mr. Carpenter slung his arms over the wagon and glanced up at the sky. "It's near time for candlelighting," he said, his voice calm once again. "No one should be traveling across this terrain in the dark. And since we can't risk the other wagon tipping over, we'll stay here tonight and make camp."

Caroline turned to her uncle, and even in the darkening shadows, she could see the same determination in his eyes that she remembered seeing so often in Father's. She knew Uncle Elisha would go for help.

"I'll go to Albert's by foot, then," Uncle Elisha said. "It can't be but a mile or two away."

"You don't know this land, Elisha," Mother said. "I say we wait until daylight. You and Joseph can go for help together."

"We'll lose a whole day of travel then, Charlotte," Mr. Carpenter said. "It's too cold for the children to be out in this night air, as it is. I say go, Quiner. And if you haven't found the homestead or some kind of help 'fore the sky's full of stars, turn around and come back. We'll keep a fire burning through the night."

"I could go along with you now, Uncle Elisha," Joseph offered.

"Thank you, son." Uncle Elisha squeezed

Joseph's shoulder. "But I'd prefer to have you here, watching out for your sisters and your mother."

"I could go, then," Henry cried out, clambering stiffly to his feet.

"You'll do no such thing," Mother said firmly.

"Let's get the wagon upright and take the wheel off," Uncle Elisha said. "I'll be back before daybreak. No lick about it."

Together they emptied the contents of the wagon onto the field. Caroline and Mother then stood back as the men tipped the wagon to its standing position. Uncle Elisha said a hurried good-bye. Carrying the cracked wagon wheel, he headed off into the dim evening light.

"A whole boodle of boys around here, and not one of them thinks of starting a fire," Mr. Carpenter exclaimed once Uncle Elisha had disappeared from sight. "Poor Caroline's cheeks are bright red with cold, and she's all ashiver!" he added. "Get to building that fire, now. Joseph, gather up some kindling!

Henry, get a flintstone and spark us up a fire!"

As the boys ran off, Mother said, "Please come help me find the bake oven and some food to cook, Caroline."

"Yes, ma'am," Caroline answered, all thoughts of the cozy homestead at Joe Albert's disappearing. Instead of setting the table in the frame house tonight, she'd help Mother cook over an open fire for the first time in her life. Instead of sleeping on her hay-stuffed mattress, she'd sleep in a hard wagon beneath the dark night sky. Caroline knew the boys thought this was a big adventure, but for her, home had never seemed so far away.

Fire Dance

Caroline pulled her quilt close around her shoulders and looked up. The stars above couldn't stay still. They bobbed up and down in the chilly night air, and the most daring stars leaped from their star settings and vaulted through the sparkling night sky.

"Hey, did you see that?" Henry said, pointing to one of the shooting stars. Seated beside Caroline by the crackling campfire, he too was watching the immense sky. "That was some pumpkins, wasn't it, Caroline! The star burned up right before our eyes!"

"Where do you think they go?" Caroline asked her brother. "Do you think the stars fall all the way to the ground?"

"I bet they make huge holes in the earth that are full of fire and starlight," Henry said.

"If I was a shooting star, I'd want to land in a field full of berries or wildflowers," Caroline decided. "Or maybe I'd drop into a dark forest and brighten it up with all my light."

"I'd fall right into the ocean," Henry said, "so I could see the fish and sea animals swimming around down there."

The grass rustled behind Caroline and Henry as Charlie and Joseph ran up to the campfire and tossed armfuls of sticks and logs to the ground with a loud thump. "This ought to be enough wood to last us a whole week," Charlie said.

"Sakes alive, gents! We could build ourselves two fires with so much kindling," Mr. Carpenter said. "You could cook us more supper, then, Charlotte," he teased.

"I'm afraid I've already cleaned and dried the bake oven, and the girls have put away all the dishes, too." Mother smiled. "I'll pour you some coffee, though, if you'd like."

"Please!" Mr. Carpenter said.

Mother used her iron tongs to lift the coffee pot off the smoking golden coals. She filled Mr. Carpenter's tin cup with coffee and poured another cup for herself. Then she sat on the wagon seat, sipped the steaming liquid, and said cheerily, "Weren't for the cold, tonight would be a perfect night for traveling. It's been years since I've cooked outdoors or slept in a wagon. You weren't even born yet, Caroline."

"No, ma'am," Caroline answered. She had been born soon after Mother, Father, Joseph, Henry, and Martha had arrived in Brookfield, Wisconsin. She had never eaten food cooked in a fire built on the ground, or slept in a wagon. Caroline had often gazed at the stars, but had never huddled outdoors with her brothers and sisters before a roaring fire, the air thick with the scents of spring blossoms and newly sprung grass, and the hearty aromas of coffee, tobacco, and burning wood.

"Supper was as tasty as anything I ever cooked on an open fire, Charlotte," Mr. Carpenter said, "and Lord knows, I've cooked plenty! Who'd ever thought I'd be eating beans from a can?"

"They came all the way from Boston," Caroline told him. "Grandmother Tucker sent them last Christmas."

"In a big trunk!" Thomas chimed in.

"I'd been saving them for the right occasion," Mother said, "and hoping they wouldn't spoil. I know beans in a can are meant to last forever, but that's just hard for me to imagine!"

"Best thing about beans in a can," Mr. Carpenter said as he stuck his pipe between his teeth, "bears can't get into them!"

"Tell your bear story, Pa," Charlie said. He dropped to the ground and sat cross-legged beside Henry.

Mr. Carpenter chuckled. "I've told that tale a thousand times, son."

"We never heard it before, Mr. Ben," Martha said.

"Tell it, please," Caroline pleaded.

Mr. Carpenter inhaled slowly on his pipe and breathed curly puffs of tobacco smoke into the night air. Then he began tapping the tip of the pipe on his knee. "I reckon I was just turned twelve years old when I met that bear," he began. "My mother had taken ill and died a year earlier. My father, plumb crazy with grief, joined her in heaven not two months later. I took his rifle and a sack of clothes and wandered through upstate New York from town to town, living with whatever shopkeeper or farmer would keep me in exchange for odd jobs. I soon grew tired of being a laborer and decided to go west. Traveling on foot mostly, I hopped on every wagon, stage, or steamship I came across that had room enough for me to hide in, or a driver kind enough to let me travel without paying. One day, I found myself in a place called Michigan. The lakes and trees were such a sight to see, I decided to stay awhile. I built a shelter out of sticks; then I turned to hunting some food. Not fifty steps away from my little hut, I found a quiet place where a flock of wild turkeys roosted. There I was, all set for food."

Seated on Mother's lap, his eyes wide with wonder, Thomas asked, "When's the bear coming?"

"Soon," Charlie assured the little boy.

"Not long after I arrived," Mr. Carpenter continued, "the weather grew cold. Snow started falling long before the last of the colored leaves had dropped from the trees. I knew I couldn't survive in such a meager dwelling, and decided to find a town and some real lodging to live in. As luck would have it, early the next morning, I heard the creaking and crunching of wagon wheels not far from my little hut. A pair of hunters had discovered the wild turkeys, and were planning to kill and sell them all."

"What'd you do, Mr. Ben?" Caroline asked.

"I decided I'd take a ride along with those hunters, figuring they were heading back to some town." Mr. Carpenter smiled. "The minute they went off to shoot the birds, I picked up my rifle and other belongings and stole through the trees to their wagon. Right behind the front bench, I found a couple of gunny sacks and some blankets. I quick climbed inside and covered myself up."

"Did the hunters find you?" Joseph asked.

"I sat quiet as a mouse beneath those blankets for what seemed like hours, listening to gunshot after gunshot, sneaking fresh air to breathe, and wondering just how many wild turkeys those hunters planned to carry back to town. Just when I thought I couldn't sit still another minute, I heard voices coming closer and was suddenly pelted with a dozen bird carcasses that were being tossed on the blankets. The hunters filled the wagon. Moments later, we moved on."

"What'd you do," Henry cried out, "covered by all those dead turkeys?"

"Well, I sat as quiet as I could, and tried not to breathe too much," Mr. Carpenter answered. "I prayed the town would be close by, and sure enough the wagon didn't go all that far before it stopped again. 'Why are you stopping here?'

I heard the first hunter ask his mate. 'There's another roost just ahead,' the second voice began. 'And there's still plenty of room back of the wagon. Might as well fill it.' Without another word, they walked off into the woods."

"Oh no!" Martha giggled. "They dropped even more turkeys on you?"

"I didn't give them a chance," Mr. Carpenter said, laughing. "I stuck my head out from beneath the blanket and pushed all those dead birds off me. Then all of a sudden, I heard a thump and a crunching in the snow, so I dove back under the birds right quick."

"What was it?" Caroline asked. She was leaning forward now, watching Mr. Carpenter intently through the leaping flames of the fire.

"I didn't rightly know, Caroline. It wasn't the hunters, I knew that. So I waited an extra minute, then stuck my head through the ceiling of turkey feathers again. That's when I met the bear." Mr. Carpenter paused. "He was standing right in front of me, his paws up to the elbow deep in turkeys."

Mother set her tin cup down on the

wagon seat next to her. "Whatever did you do, Benjamin?"

"I did the very first thing that came to mind." Mr. Carpenter chuckled. "I stood up fast as my legs would allow, threw my arms into the air, and shouted louder than I ever knew I could shout, *'EEE-YAAA!'* Well, that bear was so surprised, he up and disappeared into the forest before all the turkeys and their feathers had even dropped off my head and shoulders."

"Did you get away?" Eliza asked breathlessly.

"Faster than a woodchuck being chased by a farmer, I did. But that bear was smart as a steel trap, little Eliza, 'cause when I looked back, he was standing over the wagon again, helping himself to a whole town's autumn feast."

"Is that the only bear you ever met, Mr. Ben?" Henry asked once all the laughter ringing about the fire had quieted down.

"There's plenty more stories where that one came from, son," Mr. Carpenter answered.

"But old Thomas here looks as though he's about to fall asleep. The rest of us should get some shut-eye too, seeing how we have another day's journey facing us come sunrise. What say I help you girls into your uncle's wagon?"

"I'll be along as soon as I settle Thomas down," Mother told her daughters. "Sleep in your warm clothes and coats, and wrap yourselves tightly in your quilts."

Caroline stood up slowly. The cold wind whirling through the trees blew away the cheery warmth of the fire, and sent shivers down her spine. Following her sisters to Uncle Elisha's wagon, she listened to a pair of hoot owls conversing, their pulsing *hoo!-hoo!*s sounding hollow and lonely. Somewhere off in the trees, a wolf howled its mournful, wailing cry. Darkness filled the rest of the night, its silence immense.

"Do you suppose there are bears around here, Mr. Ben?" Caroline asked as her neighbor took her by one cold hand and helped her into the wagon. "I mean bears that like to look for food in wagons, like your bear did."

"Too much starlight for any bears to raid our wagons unnoticed tonight, little one," Mr. Carpenter said. "And if there is a frisky bear out there somewhere, he'll have to get past me, *and* this stick!"

Relieved, Caroline laughed as her friend waved a thick tree branch over his head. "Good night, Mr. Ben," she said, and climbed into the wagon.

Mother made certain Caroline, Martha, and Eliza were tucked in snugly, listened to their prayers, and kissed them good night. "I'll be back before you know it, so save me a little bit of room for sleeping, too," she said.

Once Mother had stepped off the wagon, Caroline whispered to her sisters, "If a bear comes tonight, Mr. Ben won't let him climb into our wagon. He promised."

"Is a bear coming tonight?" Eliza asked, her voice squeaking.

"No, Eliza," Martha said, "there aren't any bears here." Then she nudged Caroline. "Why are you scaring her like that?" she scolded.

"I'm trying to *un*scare her!" Caroline whispered indignantly.

"Go to sleep," Martha answered.

Caroline stared up at the twinkling black sky above. The endless dark sky hung still and silent above her. Caroline began counting stars, then fashioned shapes and animals out of the dots of light. When she discovered the outline of a great big bear, she closed her eyes tightly. Soon she drifted off to sleep.

"Caroline? Caroline!" Martha was pulling at her sleeve urgently.

Shrugging off her slumber, Caroline leaned up on her elbows. "What's wrong?" she asked.

"The howls—they're coming closer." Martha gulped, her fingers shaking as she lifted them to her lips.

Scrambling to her knees, Caroline listened. The shrill, piercing cries of wolves silenced all the night sounds of the wilderness. The cries rang out in all directions, their wailing so loud and fierce, Caroline was certain that the wagon was surrounded by the creatures.

"What's happened?" Mother sat up, her voice thick with sleep.

"Listen. It's w-wolves, Mother," Caroline stammered. "We have to get Mr. Ben. He'll keep them away."

Sitting up, Mother listened to the howls and then calmly said, "We shouldn't leave the wagon. We don't know where the wolves are."

Looking out into the darkness, Caroline glimpsed flashes of yellow that moved and disappeared into shimmering nothingness. The wolves were watching the wagon from only steps away, their yellow eyes fading in and out of view. Caroline opened her mouth to scream, but no sound came out. Instead, she heard ferocious barking and then saw Wolf bounding across the grass, leaping and barking madly.

"Wolf!" Caroline cried. "Get Mr. Ben! He's there by the campfire. Go!"

"Run, Wolf!" Martha echoed.

Eliza woke up and threw herself into Mother's arms as the earth pounded with the sound of the boys and Mr. Carpenter sprinting to the wagon. "Take one girl each!" Mr.

Carpenter was shouting and waving a tree limb he had set on fire. "Get them back to the fire and wait for me there!"

Henry reached the wagon first. "Give me Eliza," he screamed. Mother quickly lifted the sobbing little girl and handed her to Henry.

"Caroline, you're next," Joseph said urgently. "Jump! Quick!"

Caroline plunged off the side of the wagon into her brother's waiting arms. Joseph steadied her on the ground and pulled her the short distance to the fire, while Charlie reached for Martha and hurried her away from the wagon. Mr. Carpenter shouted and waved his flaming stick at the wolves as Mother climbed down from the wagon and followed the children to the campfire.

"Shhh," Mother soothed the girls as they ran into her arms. "We're all safe now."

"There's no time for talk," Mr. Carpenter cried out. "The only way we're going to send these varmints packing is to scare the devil out of them. Charlie, pull every long stick you see from that pile of wood. Joseph, light the end of each stick and give two each to your mother, Charlie, Henry, and Martha."

"I can help, too, Mr. Ben," Caroline cried out. Holding a flaming stick frightened her, but she wanted to do anything she could to make those awful eyes disappear.

"Be careful, Caroline," Mother answered. "Use both hands, and keep the fire far away from your body."

"Yes, ma'am," Caroline said, reaching out for the curved, flaming branch that Joseph handed her.

"Whirl it around, Caroline," Mr. Carpenter directed. "Make circles in the air, like this." Spinning the fireball at the end of his tree branch around and around, Mr. Carpenter painted the darkness with flaming spheres.

Caroline held onto her burning stick so tightly, the lumps and grooves in the bark dug into her skin. Slowly at first, she held her arms out straight in front of her, keeping the flames far away from her shawl. Little by little, she began moving the stick, swirling it in small circles that gradually grew larger and larger.

"Shout! Everybody!" Mr. Carpenter urged. "As loud and angry as you can!"

Ever since she was a little girl, Caroline had been told that ladies never raised their voices. But as Caroline shook her flaming stick back and forth at those yellow eyes watching her from the darkness, shrieks and whoops and hollers spilled from her tongue. Wolf bounded from side to side in front of Caroline, his bark angry and threatening.

All around the blazing fire Caroline danced and shouted with her family and the Carpenters. By the time she had burned through three sticks, Caroline could no longer see a single pair of the wolves' eyes. The howls and the wailing had disappeared as well, replaced again by the hoot owls' banter.

"I reckon we've seen the last of that pack for a while," Mr. Carpenter tossed his burned tree stubs into the fire and sighed heavily. "Thank the Lord they were loud enough to wake us," he added. Then he patted Wolf on the back. "Good work, old boy."

"I only wish Elisha had come back," Mother

worried aloud. "I hate to think of him alone in this darkness."

"We'll see him come daybreak," Mr. Carpenter said cheerfully. "Now let's catch a few winks, or we'll never be awake when he arrives. I'll get your quilts, girls. We'll all sleep near the fire for the rest of the night."

The fire leaped toward the stars as Caroline settled down on the cold earth and snuggled in between Martha and Eliza. Closing her eyes, she could still see shadows of the flickering flames and feel the safe, soothing heat on her cheeks. Mother's sweet melody soon filled the night air.

"The cuckoo is a pretty bird;
She sings as she flies.
She brings us sweet tidings;
She tells us no lies.

"She flies the mountains over;
She flies the world around.
She flies back to the mountains
And mourns for her love.

Fire Dance

"For to meet him, for to meet him,
For to meet him I will go.
For to meet my love Henry,
The young man that I love."

A *Clearing in the Woods*

"The land's just north of here, not half a mile," Uncle Elisha shouted out as Mr. Carpenter *whoa*ed his team of horses to a stop. "We'll have to cut a trace through the timber, best we can."

Caroline noticed Mr. Carpenter's brow wrinkle as he gazed into the dense forest in front of them. "If your sleigh made it through once before, the wagons ought to get by," he thought aloud. "Still, Charlotte and the children should walk behind us so they can steer clear of any sudden turnovers."

"I agree," Mother said. "We'll walk the rest of the way."

Stepping onto the dirt road and releasing Uncle Elisha's hand, Caroline waited while he helped her sisters, Mother, and Thomas down from the wagon. She glanced at the woodland before her, suddenly wanting to run away as fast and far down the territorial road as her legs would carry her. Row after row of trees faded into a gloomy forest, and no matter where Caroline looked, she didn't see any path large enough for a wagon to rumble through.

"It's exciting, isn't it?" Henry asked. Bounding up beside Caroline, he tugged at the bottom of her braid. "Somewhere on the other side of all those trees is our new house, little Brownbraid! What do you suppose it will look like?"

"I don't know," Caroline said, pulling her braid away from her brother's teasing hands. "And don't call me little Brownbraid!"

"Don't you get all huffed," Henry teased.

"I'm not huffed," Caroline shot back, resisting the urge to stamp her foot. "We slept

on the ground for three whole nights, Henry!
My dress and my shawl stink like smoke,
and so does my hair. I want to wear my nightgown and sleep in my bed. I want to sleep
in *my* room tonight, but I don't even know if
I *have* a room somewhere in all of those trees!"

"We've brought your straw tick along, and
the cabin has a room where you'll sleep,
Caroline. You need not behave so."

Caroline spun around. Mother stood there,
holding her wrapped package close against
her shawl. Caroline's cheeks flushed with
shame. She could not meet Mother's patient
eyes, but muttered, "Forgive me for complaining, ma'am."

"Every man shall bear his own burdens,
Caroline," Mother reminded her. "You won't
have to sleep on the ground tonight, but a bath
will be hard to come by until we get settled
in our new home. We can wash up before bed-
time, though. There's a river close by, out back
of our land. Soon as we get there, Henry-O, I
want you to fetch water for the cabin."

"Yes, ma'am!" Henry said. "Maybe I'll even spot us a fish for supper!"

"Time to go the whole hog!" Mr. Carpenter cried out from his wagon. "Gents! Lead the way!"

The wagons clattered and clanged, veering back and forth as Uncle Elisha and Mr. Carpenter led them slowly into the forest. Beveled rays of sunshine spilled through the trees, splashing the dried brown leaves, acorns, and rocks on the forest floor with golden light. Caroline and Eliza followed Martha and Thomas through the forest, breathing in the rich smell of pine that hung heavily in the cold forest air. A pale-green canopy of leaves towered above them as far as Caroline could see, and she soon began to wonder if she'd ever see a blue sky in this place Mother called "our new home."

"There's a clearing up ahead!" Joseph's voice rang through the still forest, and a pair of gray squirrels dashed up the trunk of the beech tree beside him.

"That's our land, then," Mother said excitedly, pointing to the still-distant clearing that was lit up with sunshine. "We've arrived!"

"May we please run ahead, Mother?" Caroline asked.

"Go," Mother said, laughing. "But stay clear of the wagons!"

Seizing Eliza's cold fingers, Caroline pulled her through piles of leaves toward the glowing light on the edge of the forest. They dashed into the clearing, then stopped. There, in a circle of sunlight, was a log house. Surrounded by dozens of tree stumps, patches of grass, tangled brush, and fallen timber, the house looked like a miniature cabin that had been dropped in the middle of an immense forest. Dark rectangles stared out of the front of the house where a door and a window should have been. A pile of logs and a wooden barrel rested against one side of the house; a stone chimney nestled against the opposite side. Behind the house, Caroline discovered a small privy and the zigzag beginnings of a rail fence. Never before had Caroline seen such a sad, lonely dwelling.

"There's no door." Eliza's small voice echoed in the quiet.

"Or windowpanes, either," Martha added, running up behind them.

"It looks smaller than our barn," Caroline said, swallowing hard.

"We *lived* in the barn before Father and Mr. Ben built us the frame house," Martha reminded her sisters. "And who says we can't build a new house? We did before. Mr. Ben and Charlie will just stay longer and help us!"

"Mother never said we were building a new house," Caroline said, her voice sharp with disappointment. "And Mr. Ben only said he was coming to help us clear the land."

"They're so big!" Eliza gasped, looking up in awe at the sugar maples, basswood, elms, oaks, and pines surrounding the log cabin. Many of the trees were wider than Uncle Elisha and Mr. Carpenter were tall. All grew up and up, towering over the little house. "How can anybody clear away all those trees?"

"We'll start by chopping up the smaller trees and removing all the brush, little Eliza," Mr.

Carpenter said as he hopped off his wagon and walked up to the girls. "Then I expect we'll cut the larger ones, or kill them by girdling. Shouldn't take us but a day or two to clear all of your mother's forty acres," he joked.

"What's girdling?" Caroline asked.

"Easier to show you than tell you," he said. Crossing to the nearest tree, Mr. Carpenter pulled his silver knife from his boot and began chipping away at the bark with the gleaming blade. His long brown hair swung back and forth across his shoulders as he peeled away the tree's rough skin with both hands. "See, Caroline, once I strip away a whole band of this bark, right here around the middle of the tree, the tree will die. We'll wait for it to come crashing down, then chop it up."

"Where will it fall?" Caroline asked, as she glanced up at all the leaves and branches shimmering in the sunlight around her.

"Wherever the good Lord wants it to," Mr. Carpenter answered. "I try my best, though, not to let any trees fall on log houses that happen to be standing nearby."

"Whoa!" Uncle Elisha brought his grunting oxen and clattering wagon to a stop at the edge of the forest. Mother and Thomas walked into the clearing behind him.

"It's smaller than I remember, Elisha," Mother said as she looked at the log cabin.

"You saw the house in the dead of winter, Charlotte, when the trees were bare," Uncle Elisha said. "It's bound to look bigger then."

Mother nodded. "Of course, you're right." She asked cheerfully, "Shall we go inside?"

"I thought I'd never get me an invite," Mr. Carpenter complained good-naturedly. "Now all I need are some peart young ladies to escort me there," he said, placing his fists on his hips and bending his knees so Caroline and Eliza could hook their arms through his. "Off we go!"

Stepping quickly through the clearing so she could keep up with Mr. Carpenter's long strides, Caroline paid little attention to anything but the maze of stumps and enormous fallen tree trunks crowding their path. She wondered how many of the toppled trees had been girdled, and how long it had taken them to die. No wonder this forest was so still.

"I'm the king of the clearing!" Henry shrieked from the far side of the house, where he was standing on top of a tree stump, waving his arms majestically in the air. "That makes the rest of you my servants!"

"Not on your life," Charlie shouted as he scrambled onto a stump that was wider and taller than Henry's. "'Cause I'm even bigger than you!"

"Maybe we could play tree-stump tag," Henry cried. Hopping down from his stump, he landed on the ground with a thump and asked, "What do you say, Joseph?" the very moment that Caroline, Eliza, and Mr. Carpenter walked up to the front of the house.

Joseph didn't answer. He was studying the chimney.

"What's the good news, Joseph?" Mr. Carpenter asked.

"Whoever built this cabin stopped building the chimney long before he finished it,"

Joseph said. "See there? It's built only as high as the roof. It sure needs to be taller, Mr. Ben."

"I'll get to it first thing, son," Mr. Carpenter assured him. "We can't take any chances with fire."

"I could help, sir," Joseph said. "Father and I built the chimney on our frame house when I was a whole lot younger."

Caroline began tapping her foot restlessly. She couldn't wait to see the inside of the cabin, and she peeked into the open doorway while Mr. Carpenter and Joseph examined the chimney.

"What's in there?" Eliza asked, wriggling past Caroline and squinting inside.

"It's too dark to see much of anything but the dirt floor," Caroline answered.

"Do you want to look inside the cabin before you find that river I told you about, Henry-O?" Mother asked, as she walked up to the house.

"I'm going to live in there for a long time, I reckon," Henry said. "I'd most like to play one game of tree-stump tag."

"Tree-stump tag can wait till you bring the water we need," Mother said. "We'll have the washstand waiting for you."

"The river's just north of here, son," Uncle Elisha told Henry, pointing toward the back of the log house. "That way, through the woods."

"Charlie, go with Henry," Mr. Carpenter said. "You can see the cabin later. And no climbing trees, you two. We've plenty of work to do before dusk."

"Yes, sir!" the boys shouted, and headed toward the woods.

"Buckets!" Mother called after them. "Don't forget the buckets in the wagon!" The boys skidded to a stop, sprinted back for the buckets, and sped off once again.

"Joseph, Elisha, let's take a look inside the house and then be on our way," Mr. Carpenter said. "After you, Charlotte, ladies." He bowed, extending his arm in front of the open door. "If you take one blink of the eye longer to look at your new home, I'll bust my boots and gallowses but good."

Giggling, Caroline, Martha, and Eliza followed Mother and a narrow stripe of sunlight into the house. Once inside, Caroline stood still until her eyes became accustomed to the dim light. She looked around the room slowly. The fireplace loomed in the center of one side wall, a large open space for a bake oven built beside it. A small black kettle hung from an iron crane in the hearth, above piles of ash and soot and charred chunks of wood. The wood box on one side was half full of logs, but the row of shelves on the opposite side of the hearth stood empty except for a single goose wing and a straw broom that leaned against the bottom shelf. Unfinished bunks were built into the back wall of the house beneath an opening for a window, and two oak planks jutted out of the other side wall, right beside a doorway that led to another room. Resting on short, split logs, the boards fashioned a long table that reached to the center of the room.

"Looks like the cabin Father built when we first came to Brookfield," Martha said.

"That cabin had a floor," Mother replied,

glancing down. The dirt floor beneath her, damp and muddy from spring rains, was sinking beneath her boots. "Your father never allowed us to move into any house or cabin until he had built us a floor."

"This house will have one too, Charlotte," Mr. Carpenter promised. "I wouldn't think of leaving you and the children here without one."

"We'll also need to build a good door right away," Uncle Elisha said. "And get some panes for the windows."

"I'm afraid the windowpanes will have to wait until we find a general store somewhere-abouts." Mr. Carpenter finished Uncle Elisha's thought. "In the meantime, we can cover the windows with deerskin."

"Couldn't we leave them open for a while?" Martha asked. "Till winter comes, at least?"

"We could change the deerskins to netting for the summer," Mr. Carpenter said. "If we can find us some netting."

"In the meantime, the hides will let plenty of light into the house, once we grease them well," Mother said. "They'll also keep mosquitoes and insects out. That's good enough, Benjamin."

As Mother spoke, Uncle Elisha crossed the room and looked up at the rafters. "Don't forget that there's a loft, Charlotte," he said. "Though it's a wonder there isn't a ladder here to climb up to it."

"Who will sleep up there?" Eliza asked.

"Your brothers, if it's built soundly enough," Mother answered. "We'll have to build a ladder for them, Elisha. Before you leave, if possible," she added.

As she turned from the loft to the empty bunks beneath the window opening, Caroline's heart sank. "None of us ever had to sleep in the big room in Brookfield," she said. "We always had bedrooms."

"We won't be sleeping in this room, Caroline," Mother said. "We'll need the extra living space those beds are taking. Instead, you and your sisters will sleep with me in that room over there," she said, pointing to the open doorway beside the table.

Quickly stepping across the soft floor, Caroline looked over Eliza's shoulder into a tiny empty room. A column of sunlight spilled through the open window onto a pool of water that sparkled back its reflection from the dirt floor.

"Too bad the gent who built this cabin didn't build some bunks into the wall of this room," Mr. Carpenter said as he laid his big warm hand on Caroline's shoulder. "We'll use the other frames, if we can, and lace them with rope to hold the ticks your mother's brought along. A morning's work is all," he predicted. "Come tomorrow night, you and your sisters will be warm and happy as three grizzlies in the thick of a winter's freeze."

"Yes, sir." Though her throat felt tight, Caroline managed to speak. But she couldn't bring herself to look up at Mr. Carpenter, and stared down at the flashing puddle instead.

"Here's water!" Henry's shout suddenly bounced about the walls of the little log house.

Squeezing Caroline's shoulder gently, Mr. Carpenter said, "I'm off to find your mother's

washstand and basin, Miss Caroline. The
sooner this house starts looking like a home,
the sooner it will start feeling like one!"

"Please, Benjamin, Elisha," Mother said,
"bring the stove first, then some pots and pans,
and some flour and utensils. A hot meal will
boost all of our spirits."

Crossing to the hearth, she carefully unwrapped her candlesticks and placed them on
the crude wooden mantel above the fireplace.
"There!" Mother said happily. "Our little cabin
is beginning to look like home already."

"We'll bring your stove, Charlotte," Uncle
Elisha said, grinning, "but no more of your
fine furnishings until Carpenter and I build
you that floor."

Joseph built a roaring fire in the hearth.
Mother mixed fresh corn bread batter and
poured it in the bake kettle above the leaping flames of the fire. Once a second fire
blazed in the stove, Mother heated her last
cans of Boston baked beans and pickled cauli-
flower. Caroline and Martha sorted through
the dishes and utensils until they found the

proper place settings, and carefully set the long oak table. Then they waited for their turns to wash.

When Eliza stepped away from the washbasin, Caroline immediately dipped her hands into the cold fresh water, splashing it over her cheeks and head. She scrubbed her hands and face with the soft soap that Mother had set out, rinsed, scrubbed, and rinsed again. When Caroline finally sat down at the crowded table, she felt cleaner, but she couldn't help wishing that she could soak in a warm tub of water. Still, with a set table, the aroma of beans and corn bread filling the air, and a cheery fire in the hearth, the cabin *was* beginning to feel more like a home.

"We thank Thee, Lord, for the blessing of this new house and land," Mother began praying aloud, "and ask for patience and strength as we settle into it."

"Amen," Caroline said, and she ate every bite of her supper.

After supper, Uncle Elisha laid the girls' mattress on a thick blanket in a corner of their new bedroom. Caroline smoothed the straw that had bunched up inside the linen tick, helped Eliza dress for bed, then dressed herself.

Mother joined her daughters for prayers and answered each "good night" with a kiss on the forehead. "Till Mr. Carpenter moves the bed frames from the other room or builds us new ones, we'll keep this blanket beneath the mattress and hope we don't get any rain," she said. Smiling wryly, she added, "We'd have to float to our dreams, then."

Caroline tossed and turned, trying to get comfortable. The straw inside the tick was old and broken, and couldn't make the hard floor feel anything but hard.

"I wish I could stay out there in the big room and listen to all of Mr. Ben's stories," Martha said. "Tomorrow I'll ask Mother if I can," she decided. "I'm almost as old as Henry, after all." Turning her back to Eliza, who was lying between her sisters in the middle of the mattress, Martha sighed heavily, and she soon drifted off to sleep.

The tiny room was quiet. Voices talked and

teased in the larger room next door. Mother continued to hush them. The world outside the window hole remained dark and silent, but for the whooshing of the wind and the occasional cries of a lone wolf.

"Do you like it here, Caroline?" Eliza whispered.

Caroline didn't answer. Hugging her pillow tightly, she stared out the dark window opening, biting her lip and wishing that the moon would appear and brighten the darkness.

"I don't," Eliza continued. "I wish . . ." Her voice quivered, and she stopped speaking as her little body began to shake with sobs.

Caroline wrapped her arms around Eliza, hugging her close. "It's all right," she whispered, her own sadness forgotten as she comforted Eliza. "Uncle Elisha and Mr. Ben will make this house a whole lot better than it is now. Just think, Eliza—we don't even know what else there is to see around here. Maybe we can go find the river tomorrow," Caroline said, trying her best to sound excited. "Henry and Charlie say it's as pretty as any river they've ever seen!"

Caroline held her sister for a long time, stroking the long, soft curls that had escaped from her nightcap. When Eliza's shoulders finally stopped shaking, and her breathing became steady and sound, Caroline settled back on her side of the mattress. A string of heavenly lights now flickered outside the window hole. She rested her head on her pillow and watched the winking stars. Mother and Father had surely slept on dirt floors in cabins without windows. They had built crude cabins and turned them into homes. Mother and Father had moved from place to place in the wilderness, only to see new towns spring up wherever they settled. Closing her eyes, Caroline knew that Mother would make this cabin a home and settle this wilderness, too. As she drifted off to sleep, Caroline promised herself she would help.

Beds and Braids

While Uncle Elisha built a heavy oak door, Mr. Carpenter constructed two large bed frames for the girls and Mother. When it was time to make the springs, he called the girls into the small bedroom to watch. Holding on to a thick coil of rope, he pulled it tautly up and down and from side to side over each frame, lacing the beds. When Mr. Carpenter finished, both frames were crosshatched with row after row of little rope squares.

Leaning over the beds, Mr. Carpenter pressed firmly on the rope squares with both hands. "Until I have the time to whittle some pegs and finish these beds proper," he said, "you can walk on these springs whenever they start to sag, and shift 'em around with your feet until the sag is all gone!"

"Yes, sir!" Eliza sang out.

"May we try it now?" Caroline couldn't help asking.

Mr. Carpenter laughed. "Why not?"

In their bare feet, Caroline and Eliza climbed up on the beds and began teetering across the rope springs.

"Watch that you don't get a toe or two stuck beneath the ropes," Mr. Carpenter reminded the girls as they moved from square to square.

Arms extended to keep her balance, Caroline stepped from square to square, shifting the ropes until they were straight and tight beneath her. Then she hopped off the bed, pulled the mattress on top of the new springs, and smoothed out the bunched-up straw.

"It's perfect, Mr. Ben!" Caroline cried.

Reaching for one end of their thick quilt, she and Martha lifted it high above the straw tick and let it slowly settle on their new bed.

Mr. Carpenter beamed. "Now it's high time your uncle and I get to planking the floors. If your mother doesn't need you in the cabin, ladies, you might ask to help your brothers and Charlie. All the brush and saplings around the house must be cleared away 'fore we can start chopping down the big trees and turn the ground over for planting."

Martha happily agreed. "We'll ask Mother this minute!" she exclaimed.

Caroline wasn't nearly as excited as Martha. Henry and Charlie had been clearing away brush all morning, and had come to dinner with their hands and wrists aching and their shirts and trousers covered with dirt, twigs, and leaves. Glancing at the new beds Mr. Carpenter had spent a whole morning building, however, Caroline felt ashamed that she didn't want to help.

"I'll pull up as much brush as I can, Mr.

Ben," she said. "Thank you for making us these fine beds."

"You're as welcome as a spring day in December," Mr. Carpenter said, smiling.

Poking her head in through the open doorway, Mother examined the two new beds, her eyes shining. "They certainly look wonderful," she said. "I have half a mind to wish this day away, so I can go right to sleep!"

"Mr. Ben asked us to help the boys," Martha burst out. "May we go outside now, Mother?"

Mother turned to Mr. Carpenter. "Help cutting trees?" she asked, surprised.

"The boys are cutting down the saplings and brush and such. They need help dragging them into one big pile for burning. If it's all right with you, Charlotte, the girls can do that," Mr. Carpenter answered matter-of-factly. Then his voice grew more serious. "The corn and potatoes must be planted now or you won't have crops to feed you for the next year. The sooner the brush is cleared, the sooner Elisha and I can take down the big trees and pull the roots and stumps from the field so we can plant. Six pairs of hands are much better than three, Charlotte, but if you'd rather not have the girls working in such a way. . . ." He hesitated.

"I don't see that we have any other choice," Mother said, relenting. "I'm just thankful that your grandmother Tucker isn't here to see you girls working in the fields like hired hands. Help your brothers and Charlie the best you can. I'll send for you when it's time to get supper."

As she stepped into the warm spring afternoon, Caroline fingered the folds of her dress. The wool was still brown, though a much paler shade than it had been when Martha had first worn the dress years ago. The fabric was less scratchy, and most of the stains that had marred the sleeves and collar had faded with the color. Caroline's apron was now a dingy gray, and as she lifted it away from her dress, she couldn't help wishing it were still crisp and white, as it had been when Mother had first made it for Martha.

"I bet you're thinking about your dress and

how dirty it's going to get if we help Charlie and the boys," Martha said, watching her sister. She stopped suddenly in front of Caroline. The afternoon sun was shining through her loose braids, and the brown wisps blowing about her face shone like copper. "That's just what you're thinking, Caroline," Martha insisted. "Say so if it's true!"

Stunned, Caroline released the folds of her apron and skirt. The gritty wool fell against her bare legs, covering them with itches. "How do you know what I'm thinking?" she shot back.

"What does it matter if your clothes are torn, or your precious apron gets stained?" Martha asked. "You don't have a school to go to anymore, or friends to see in town. Who knows if there's even a town close enough to visit? No one's going to notice your dress, no matter what it looks like."

"Be quiet, Martha," Eliza spoke up. "Or I'll tell Mother you're bullying Caroline."

"You don't have to talk for me, Eliza," Caroline quickly countered without taking her eyes off her older sister. "Seems to me you're the one who should be most wanting to look nice, Martha, since Charlie's come to stay with us," she said. "Too bad your hair is more out of your braids than in them, and your face and hands are never clean. Even your dress looks old and crumpled. If I was Charlie, I wouldn't look at you twice!"

The moment the last spiteful word slipped from her tongue, Caroline lifted her fingers to her lips. She wished that she could take back every word, but their horrible sound was still ringing in her ears. "I . . . I'm sorry," she stammered as she watched a single tear slide down Martha's pale cheek. "I should never have said any of it."

"I said, 'Say so if it's true,'" Martha replied, wiping her cheek. "You just told the truth, is all."

"Stop it!" Eliza cried out. "Stop it right now!"

"I'm going to help Mother with supper," Martha said.

"No, Martha!" Caroline pleaded. "You have

to come and help us. You promised Mr. Ben."

Martha turned and ran as quickly as she could back to the log house without another word.

Eliza looked up at Caroline, her eyes wide with wonder. "I never heard you talk like that before," she said.

"Let's go help the boys," Caroline answered, ignoring Eliza's comment.

Caroline and Eliza wove their way around dozens of chopped-off tree trunks and were soon standing in front of the boys in a patch of clearing that was littered with small trees, large rocks, and brush. Saplings lay strewn about, their young branches covered with freshly budded leaves, their green roots neatly severed. All about them, young pine trees lay fallen over on their sides.

Joseph swung a final blow into a maple that was only a head taller than he was, rested his axe on the ground, and swiped the back of his arm across his forehead. "What's happened, Caroline?" he shouted above the cracking of Henry's and Charlie's axes.

"Mr. Ben's sent us to help pile the trees you cut down for burning," Caroline answered.

Joseph raised an eyebrow suspiciously. "Does Mother know about this?" he asked.

"Yes." Eliza nodded, her yellow braids bouncing about her shoulders.

"Fine, then," Joseph said. "We could use the help. Charlie's already started a pile over there. Drag the trees over to him, and just move on to another tree if one's too hard to get hold of."

"You pull the brush and other such small things, Eliza," Caroline said. "I'll take the trees." Pushing her sleeves up to her elbows, she bent down in front of a fallen pine tree and grabbed the small trunk around its prickly, gummy base. Inching her way backward, Caroline pulled the tree along, glancing over her shoulder every few steps to make certain that she wasn't about to trip or bump into something. When she finally arrived at Charlie's pile, her arms were already tingling, and her back ached from walking hunched over.

"'Oh, Susanna!'" Charlie sang out happily as Caroline dropped the tree trunk she was holding beside the pile. "'Oh don't you cry for me!' 'Cause I got just what I want and need . . ." Finishing his song, Charlie yelped, "Two more helpers!"

Giggling, Caroline looked up into Charlie's sparkling eyes. His face was damp with sweat and streaked with dirt, but he was still handsome. And kind and funny, too. No wonder Martha liked Charlie so much.

"So where's Miss Martha?" Charlie asked, pushing his black hair out of his eyes. "Three helpers would be even better than two."

Caroline's cheeks grew hot with shame at the mention of her sister's name, and she quickly looked away. "Martha stayed back at the cabin to help Mother," she said. "I'm going for more trees."

"You bring 'em, I'll string 'em!" Charlie cried, and then he burst into another made-up stanza of "Oh, Susanna!" Caroline hurried back to the place where Henry and Joseph were busily hacking down trees, and reached for another young sapling. Back and forth she crossed that small stretch of land, dragging tree after tree to Charlie's pile, determined to clear away enough trees for both her and Martha. It seemed after a time that all she had done her whole life was to clear trees, one by one by one.

Finally, the unmistakable clanging of a wooden spoon against an iron pot rang out across the clearing. Dropping her last pine tree beside Charlie's burning pile, Caroline looked toward the cabin and found Mother waving them in for supper. Hands shaky, stained with dirt, and covered with pine needles and bits of stone, she rubbed them together gently, blowing on them.

"'Zooks, Caroline! You cleared away more trees than Joseph and I could have together," Henry said with admiration as he caught up with Caroline and Eliza on their way back to the house. "I hope Mother lets you out of the house to work with us every day!"

Caroline tried to smile at Henry, but she was too tired. Her back ached, and her legs felt so wobbly, she wasn't even certain they would carry her the last few steps to the house.

"It's a wonder Martha wasn't out here helping instead of you and Eliza," Henry continued, his voice lowered. "I'd a thought she'd do just about anything to spend more time with Charlie, having set her cap for him the way she has."

"She wanted to help more than anybody," Eliza informed her big brother. "Till she and Caroline got in a big fight, anyway."

"Hush, Eliza," Caroline said quickly.

Stepping into the dimly lit house, Caroline quickly looked around for her older sister. Mother was busy at the stove; Mr. Carpenter and Uncle Elisha were pounding floorboards in a far corner of the room. Thomas knelt beside them, his little hands full of pegs. Martha was nowhere to be found.

"Wash up quickly, children," Mother said. "Supper's near ready."

Caroline waited her turn, then dipped her sore hands into the washbasin and soaked them in the water. Gingerly she splashed water over her hot cheeks and steaming forehead.

"Goodness glory!" Mother exclaimed as Caroline dried her face and hands. "You are a sight to see, Caroline. I expect we'll need to wash and wring that dress and apron two or three times before we have even half a chance of seeing their right color again. And whatever happened to your sleeve, child? The seam is nearly ripped off your shoulder."

"You should have seen her work," Henry said proudly as he looked up from the washbasin, his face dripping wet. "She nearly built Charlie's burning pile all by herself!"

Shaking her head, Mother spoke beneath her breath. "It's a disgrace, young girls like you working at such tasks. I have half a mind to put us all in that wagon and drive back to Brookfield, house or no house!"

Caroline looked down at her clothes. Her dress and apron were even dirtier than the boys' clothes had been earlier that day at dinner. Her sleeve was ripped at the shoulder, and her hem hung unevenly where it had been snagged and torn in two different places. "I was trying to help the boys the best I could," Caroline said. "I forgot all about my dress, but I can help you wash it, if you like. I can even mend the hem if you help me."

"Pay me no mind, little one," Mother said. "You should be proud of all your hard work." Kneeling in front of Caroline, she rubbed her sore hands. "These first weeks will be especially trying, is all, and we must help each other through them. I'll mend your dress tonight, Caroline, and clean it as soon as possible."

Nodding, Caroline thanked Mother. "Where's Martha?" she finally asked.

"She's resting in the back room," Mother answered. "She was complaining of a sick stomach, so I told her to rest. Please go see if she's hungry for supper, Caroline."

Caroline slowly walked into the back room. Martha was lying on their new bed, facing the wall. Caroline wanted to crawl right onto the mattress beside her sister and fall asleep at once. Instead, she said softly, "It's time for supper, Martha."

"I don't want any supper."

Caroline stood there a moment. When she finally spoke, her words tumbled out so quickly, she scarcely heard herself saying them. "Charlie's having supper with us, and seeing how he kept asking why you didn't come help drag the trees, I think you should at least come to supper."

Rolling over on her side, Martha looked at Caroline, her brown eyes glowing. "I guess I should eat then, shouldn't I?" she asked. Then she looked more closely at her younger sister. "You're a sight, Caroline," she said.

Sitting down on the edge of the mattress, Caroline sighed and looked at her red, scratched hands. "You would have helped a lot today," she said simply. "He's nice, I think. Charlie is. I'll tell Mother you're coming to supper," she added, and she stood up to leave the room.

"Caroline?" Martha called out from the bed, stopping Caroline in midstep. Reaching for the brush that was set on the bureau between the two beds, Martha held it up.

"You make the tightest braids of anybody, except Grandma," she said.

Caroline walked back to the bed and took the brush from her sister. "One braid or two?" she asked, as she loosened Martha's braids and smoothed out her sister's soft hair.

"One today," Martha answered. "I always wear two."

Caroline twisted and tucked Martha's hair into the tightest, prettiest braid she had ever made. Together, she and her sister joined the others for supper.

Charlie was the first to notice Martha's new hairstyle. "Look at you, all fixed up for supper," he said. "Makes me almost want to change into my Sunday clothes."

Martha looked down at her bowl of cold succotash. Her cheeks flushed brightly. "Thank you, Charlie," she said, and she reached beneath the table to give Caroline's fingers a grateful squeeze.

Tricks

The pink, white, and purple hepaticas brightening the woodlands bloomed briefly, then withered on their hairy stems. Stalks of shining mayflowers and vivid clumps of wild blue phlox dabbled color through the forest. Cool breezes breathed fresh air across the land, carrying away the acrid smells of burning timber and brushwood that hung thickly over the clearing.

On May's first bright morning, Caroline was shooing her chickens back into the small chicken coop Uncle Elisha had built. Gently nudging the rooster into the wooden box with her broom, she pulled the door shut amid clucks and squawks of protest.

"If it makes you feel any better, I miss your old henhouse, too," she called out through the closed door as she leaned her broom against it. Rubbing the dirt off her hands, which were now callused and strong from weeks of clearing the land, she added, "I mostly wish you still had a whole row of nesting boxes, so I wouldn't have to search all over for your eggs! Mother says I should stop letting you scatter, and then you'll have to lay your eggs in this coop. We'll try it her way tomorrow morning; what do you say?"

Caroline knew full well that come daybreak, she'd arrive at the little coop, pull the door open, and let the birds strut outside to nibble and peck at their feed in the fresh morning air. "Well, I wouldn't want to be kept in that little box all day and night, either," she said to the chickens. Circling the coop, she tried to recall where the broody hens had disappeared earlier this morning, when she had set them free. Carefully, she combed through each thick patch of grass and wildflowers she remembered seeing a hen dart into, gingerly feeling around for any eggs that might have been laid there.

Moments later Caroline wrapped her fingers around a warm egg that was nestled in a soft bed of leaves and grass. "This must be the last one," she said happily. She was placing the egg gently into her basket when she suddenly heard voices behind her. Uncle Elisha and Mr. Carpenter were standing beside a white pine whose pointed crown pierced the heavens.

"Grub out the stumps before we plant, you think?" Uncle Elisha was asking.

"They'll rot soon enough," Mr. Carpenter answered. "I say we put in around them."

Uncle Elisha looked around the clearing, imagining what he would be planting if the field in front of him were his garden. "Will we have the space we need, Carpenter? We have to seed enough food to last Charlotte's family until next year, mind you."

"We've done cleared 'most an acre, Elisha. There's no more time for clearing land," Mr. Carpenter replied. "I'll get these last two trees down, if they'll fall free of the house; then we'll get to planting. Come week's end, Charlie and I go back to Brookfield. We have to get our own crops into the ground 'fore it's too late."

"What about the barn?" Uncle Elisha asked. "We've saved all those logs to build it."

"The logs will keep out back of the house. And if they don't, there are plenty more trees to use when we're ready to build. Except for the hens, Charlotte has no animals to keep inside come winter. No hay or feed, neither," Mr. Carpenter continued. "Will be another spring 'fore she gets herself a feeder or heifer. Good Lord willing, the boy and I will come back this fall to build a barn with Joseph and Henry. Otherways, it can wait till spring."

Standing straight up, Caroline was about to plead, "Please don't go! Not yet! We need a barn, and a bigger henhouse!" But she closed her mouth as soon as she opened it. Mr.

Carpenter, Charlie, and Uncle Elisha had been with them nearly three weeks. She knew they had to return to their families. Caroline just hadn't realized there would still be so much to do after they left.

"Are you going to measure 'fore we take these trees down," Uncle Elisha asked, "or shall I?"

"No sense in dropping them on those new plank floors, heh?" Mr. Carpenter joked. "I'll do the measuring if you'll round up the boys and start them turning over the ground. I've one or two grub hoes in the wagon if need be."

Caroline looked at the only two trees still standing near the log house. The first, a sugar maple, grew a short distance away from the chimney, its lofty branches dangling over the roof. The second tree, a mighty oak, stood farther away, towering over the landscape of dotted tree stumps. Its gray shadow stretched across the clearing, darkening the front of the house. Caroline couldn't imagine how the oak tree could possibly miss the house if it tumbled to the ground; its shadow was already falling on it. Lifting her basket of eggs carefully, she walked over to Mr. Carpenter, who was pounding a stick into the ground.

"Pardon me, Mr. Ben, but won't that tree fall right on our house if you cut it down?" she inquired.

"I don't rightly know, Caroline," Mr. Carpenter replied. His dark eyes crinkled at the corners as he smiled down at her. "I'm planning to measure it and see, though. Care to help?"

"Yes, sir," Caroline answered, setting her basket of eggs on a tree stump behind her.

"The trick is to figure out the length of this stick. Let's say for our purposes it's one length long," he began. "Next, we need to measure the stick's shadow. Here's another rod, Caroline, same size as the first," he said, handing it to her. "Why don't you see how many times you can fit this rod into the other stick's shadow."

Reaching for the rod, Caroline placed it on the ground beside the stick's long shadow. With her bare toe, she marked the shadow where the rod ended, then lifted it up and placed it over the rest of the shadow that fell on the other side of her toe. "The stick's shadow is two rods long, Mr. Ben."

"So now we know that the shadows this time of day are twice as long as the object they're shadowing," Mr. Carpenter reasoned. "Now, all we have to measure is the tree's shadow, and take away half its length. Then we'll know just how tall our tree really is!"

Climbing onto the twisted, rolling roots of the oak tree, Mr. Carpenter leaned one end of the rod against the base of the tree and then set it on the ground. Turning the rod over on itself again and again, he followed the tree's shadow across the clearing, counting each time he flipped the rod until he arrived at the side of the house where the tip of the tree's shadow shaded the ground. "Forty-four lengths," he told Caroline as he walked back to the tree. "Half of that is twenty-two lengths. Is that right?"

Caroline had only just begun practicing sums before she left Brookfield and hadn't yet learned how to take half away from anything. Not knowing for certain how to answer Mr. Carpenter's question, she replied simply, "It sounds right, sir."

"Good," Mr. Carpenter agreed. "Now we need to measure the distance from the tree to the house. If it's twenty-two lengths or shorter, we'll have to leave the old hardwood where it stands."

Walking along behind Mr. Carpenter, Caroline counted each flip of the rod as he determined the distance between tree and house. The moment they were standing before the front door, Mr. Carpenter turned back to Caroline and slapped his knee jubilantly. "Twenty-seven lengths!" he exclaimed. "We've got ourselves a tumbler!"

"Will you girdle it, sir?" Caroline asked, proudly speaking the new word.

"Takes too long for it to die that way," Mr. Carpenter replied, shaking his head. "I need to chop it up and have the oxen haul the trunks away before Elisha drives the team back to Milwaukee. I'll start cracking through it today. Plenty of room to swing my axe now that we've done so much clearing."

"Caroline?" Mother poked her head out the door. "I thought I heard your voice. Did you collect the eggs yet?"

"Yes, ma'am. I found four," Caroline replied, with a quick glance back at the old oak tree. Dozens of stumps surrounded the base of the tree. Caroline quickly scanned them, trying to locate the stump where she'd set her basket. But she didn't see it anywhere. "I'll bring them inside right away," she promised.

"Fine. Uncle Elisha needs you and your sisters to help the boys begin planting," Mother told her. "After you bring me the eggs, please go see if the potatoes we're rooting have split and sprouted yet."

"Yes ma'am," Caroline answered, and she dashed back toward the oak tree.

The bright green leaves of the old oak were fluttering in the breeze as Caroline climbed onto its roots. "I was standing right there when we started measuring," she murmured, looking over at the stick that Mr. Carpenter had driven into the ground. "I put my basket on the stump behind me, I remember," she added, turning to face the sawed-off trunk growing directly behind the measuring stick.

Hopping off the roots, Caroline ran over to the stump and looked it over from top to bottom. Except for the hodgepodge of ants milling in aimless circles across the middle of the barren stub, Caroline didn't see anything. She walked around the warm grass a second time, searching for her basket and the four fresh eggs that she now feared might have tumbled out of it.

"O-o-o-wah! O-o-o-wah!"

A loud cackle rippled through the trees. Caroline whirled around, her skin bumping up with prickles. "Who's there?" Caroline called, wondering if the odd sound came from some strange animal she'd never seen before.

"O-o-o-wah! O-o-o-wah!" the shrill noise bleated again.

Treading cautiously toward the band of trees

that edged the clearing, Caroline looked high up into their tangle of branches. Was it a bird? A crow, maybe? A pile of dry leaves crackled beneath a heavy footstep, and Caroline stood frozen in place. Someone else was walking nearby. Turning back toward the house, she searched for Mr. Carpenter, but he was nowhere to be seen. "Who's there?" she called out again.

A hand dangling a basket from its gray fingertips suddenly shot out from behind the trunk of an elm tree in front of Caroline. "Looking for these?" a low voice growled as a gray face poked out above the hand. A mop of dirty curls topped the face, and two piercing blue eyes surrounded by white rings stared down at Caroline. *"O-o-o-wah!"*

Unable to decide whether she should run away or stay and fight for her eggs, Caroline looked into the blue eyes across from her, her heart pounding. The eyes looked familiar, she thought as she stared back at them.

"Those are my eggs," she called out as firmly as she could. "Put the basket down, and go away so I can come get them."

"Mine!" the voice howled back. *"O-o-o-wah!"*

The blue eyes looked straight into Caroline's, and she suddenly realized they were laughing merrily at her. It's Henry, she thought, glancing at the curls bobbing about the gray face as her brother howled up at the sky.

"Give me back my eggs!" she yelled.

Henry laid the basket of eggs on the ground and burst into a fit of laughter. Caroline discovered another boy chortling hysterically from a tree beside her brother. His face, hands, clothes, and hair were a fuzzy dark gray, too. It was Charlie.

"These two bothering you, Caroline?" a man's voice said from behind.

Whirling around, Caroline found Mr. Carpenter standing there, the barrel of his musket resting on the ground beside his leg. She could tell from the angry look in Mr. Carpenter's eyes that Henry and Charlie were in big trouble. "No, sir," she quickly answered.

"Stealing a little girl's eggs, howling like wolves, and laughing like a bunch of hyenas,"

Mr. Carpenter said. "Seems to me they're causing all sorts of trouble."

"It's Henry, Mr. Ben!" Caroline said. "And Charlie, too."

Mr. Carpenter stood still, his gaze unwavering. "Why, it couldn't possibly be Charlie and Henry. They're over by the burning pile, collecting barrels of ash to sell in town," he said. "Besides, no son of mine would knowingly scare a child half out of her wits."

"We *were* dumping the ash into the barrels," Henry said earnestly. "That's how we got ourselves all dirty."

"We didn't mean nothing by our fooling," Charlie said.

"Well, I'll be a-knocked into a cocked hat!" Mr. Carpenter whistled low between his teeth. "If it isn't my son and his good friend Henry Quiner. Apologize to this young lady for taking her eggs, then get yourselves cleaned up or I'll tan your hides! We've an acre of land to seed before week's end, and not one more minute to waste on tomfoolery."

"Yes, sir," Charlie spoke up first. "Sorry,"

he told Caroline, then dashed off to the river.

"I wish I never did it," Henry whispered into Caroline's ear. Squeezing her shoulders, he added, "You were real brave, Caroline."

"Best you get those eggs to your mother," Mr. Carpenter said, once Henry had disappeared.

"Yes, sir," Caroline said. Stepping across the warm grass, she picked up her basket of eggs, peeked inside to see if any were broken, then turned back to Mr. Carpenter, who was pulling his measuring stick out of the ground. "How'd you know I was in trouble, Mr. Ben?" she asked.

"I didn't," he acknowledged, grinning. "I was heading back here to get this rod, and heard that awful cackling. I got hold of my musket and came to take a look. That's when I discovered Charlie and Henry making a terrible nuisance of themselves."

"You knew all along it was them?" Caroline cried, her eyes wide with surprise.

"A man knows his son no matter how hard he tries to hide himself," Mr. Carpenter explained. "Though sometimes he might not want to admit it." Placing his hand on Caroline's shoulder, he steered her back toward the little log house.

"I wish you and Charlie could stay here with us, Mr. Ben," Caroline said softly.

"You'll see me again soon, little one," Mr. Carpenter said, his voice as gentle as his touch. With a heavy sigh, he added, "But how Brookfield will miss the peart Quiner girls!"

Caroline wanted to tell Mr. Carpenter how much she would miss him, and how thankful she was that he and Uncle Elisha had turned the unfinished cabin into a warm, safe house. But her words were suddenly stuck in her throat. Watching her bare feet press down the bright-green grass, she walked back to the house slowly, Mr. Carpenter's warm hand now heavy on her shoulder.

When they arrived at the door, Caroline set her basket of eggs on the ground and gave her friend a hug. From the look in his suspiciously bright eyes, she knew that Mr. Carpenter knew what she couldn't find the words to say.

Shanty

"Why are we planting pumpkins on top of corn?" Eliza asked, fingering the smooth green leaves of the just-sprouted corn plants. "These leaves are so little, the pumpkins will squish them good."

"We aren't going to plant the pumpkin seeds on top of the corn," Caroline explained. She swept her bare toes through a hill of dirt and covered the seeds she'd just sprinkled in a freshly dug hole. "We're going to plant the pumpkin seeds around the corn. Their big leaves and vines will stop weeds that choke the corn from growing."

"Mr. Ben said to be sure and plant beans and squash around the corn, too," Martha reminded her sisters. She shaped some soil into a small hill and added, "Mr. Ben says they'll protect the corn every bit as good as the pumpkins. We shouldn't forget."

Caroline looked at Eliza and rolled her eyes. Ever since Mr. Carpenter and Uncle Elisha had left three weeks ago, Martha had been reminding them daily about each instruction Mr. Carpenter had given. Stranger still, rather than begging to help Joseph and Henry outside, she now spent most of her days happily helping Mother with indoor chores. Most worrisome of all, Martha insisted on having her long hair neatly braided every morning, and for the first time that Caroline could ever remember, her older sister was suddenly very particular about keeping her clothes and shoes free from dirt and stains. Martha still looked the same, although a bit neater. But Caroline couldn't help wondering if there just might be some new person stuck inside her sister.

"Girls?" Mother called out from the front of the house, shielding her eyes from the sun's glare.

Martha jumped up. "Yes, ma'am?" she called back.

"Leave the rest of the planting until this afternoon. I need one of you to go tell the boys it's near time for dinner, and another to come inside and set the table."

"I'll go help Mother," Martha told her sisters. Clapping clumps of dirt off her hands, she directed, "You go get the boys, Caroline. Take Eliza with you."

"Yes, ma'am!" Caroline exclaimed, shutting her mouth quickly before she snapped at her sister for being so bossy. "I'd rather stay outside awhile longer, anyway," she said to Martha's back as she watched her step importantly toward the house, her neat braids swinging.

Pouring her pumpkin seeds into Caroline's open hand, Eliza remained quiet as Caroline dropped the seeds into the deepest corners of her apron pocket. "Martha sure is acting funny," she finally said. "She never likes it when Joseph or Henry tell *her* what to do, so how come she keeps telling *us* what to do?"

"Never mind her," Caroline advised. "I think she's mostly sad on account of Charlie leaving. I'm ready to go now. Come, Wolf," she called to the dog, who was resting his long furry face in the shade of a thick tree stump. Wolf rose to his feet the moment Caroline beckoned, and he was soon prancing along at their side.

The sun pulsed behind a film of gleaming white heat, beating through their bonnets and calico dresses as Caroline and Eliza ran across the clearing. Rushing into the dappled shade of the forest, they crossed to the woodpile where Joseph was splintering a thick log into wood for the fire.

"Where's Henry?" Caroline called out over the loud cracking of iron against wood.

"He went to the river to clean Thomas," Joseph answered. Wiping his shirtsleeve across his sweaty face, he grinned and added, "Thomas helped fill the wood box for the first time today, and by the time he was finished, he was wearing more dirt and wood chips than clothes."

"Mother says it's near time for dinner," Caroline said. Leaning over, she pulled a thin sliver of wood out of the callused sole of her foot. "Ouch," she complained.

"I can finish breaking this trunk apart if you girls get Henry and Thomas," Joseph said. "It won't take but a few minutes more."

Caroline watched a tiny crack in her skin bubble with bright-red blood where she'd yanked out the sliver. "Which way did they go?" she asked absentmindedly.

"They went out straight back of the house," Joseph answered. "It's quicker to the river from there."

Caroline couldn't wait to dip her sore foot into the cool river water. "Let's go, Eliza," she said.

Limping over the speckled red leaves and runners of wild strawberry plants blooming on the edge of the forest, Caroline led the way to the river. Sunlight fluttered through a lush canopy of leaves, its blazing heat cooled by the moist, shady woods. Woodpeckers flew from elm to elm, their wings beating, then stretching into a silent, tranquil glide. Gray squirrels bobbled about, feasting on the clusters of wild mushrooms that crowded in the holes of rotted logs.

"Look, Eliza!" Caroline cried. A buckeye butterfly flittered past. It landed on the trunk of a silver maple and proudly displayed the brilliant blue dots and feathery orange stripes trimming its wings.

"It's so pretty!" Eliza breathed, standing on her tiptoes to get a better look.

"I never saw a place so beautiful," Caroline whispered. "Just think, Eliza, it's all ours!"

No longer in a hurry, Caroline and her younger sister strolled along, listening to the harmonies lilting through the fresh, piney air: the chirping, crunching, and flapping that perked up the wilderness. Marveling at the spectacular landscape before her, Caroline said, "It's like no one else is alive in this whole wide world."

Eliza nodded without saying a word. Even Wolf was quiet, panting softly. "We should find the boys now," Caroline said at last. "Mother will wonder what's taking us so long."

"How much farther to the river, do you think?" Eliza asked.

"It's up just a ways, I can hear it," Caroline said, squinting to see the farthest point of the forest. The riverbank was not yet in view. Up ahead, Caroline noticed, was a small shelter. "What do you suppose that is, Eliza?" she asked, pointing toward the shack.

Eliza shrugged. "Looks like a little house," she answered. "Who do you think lives there?"

"Mother never said anything about someone else living on our land," Caroline said doubtfully. "I think we should go see who's there."

Wolf growled low in his throat as Eliza sputtered, "We should wait. Let's go get Henry and Thomas, and bring them back here with us."

Caroline considered Eliza's plan for a moment, then decided against it. "We have to

pass the hut on our way to the river, anyway,"
she reasoned. "There's no smoke coming out
of the chimney, for goodness' sakes. It'd be a
wonder if anyone was living there at all."

Reaching for her sister's hand, Caroline
pulled her through the woods, Wolf still growling as they came to the tiny shanty. A tilted
roof, covered with dried leaves and pine
branches, topped the four log walls. A chimney was built into one side of the shanty, and
the door in front was nearly as tall as the
dwelling itself. Caroline stopped and whispered into Eliza's ear, "The door's partly open.
Let's just peek inside real quick."

"You go." Eliza spoke so softly, Caroline almost couldn't hear her words.

Caroline looked at Eliza's pale, worried face.
"Stay here with Wolf. I'll be right back."

Leaves crunching beneath her bare feet,
Caroline walked right up to the door and
peered into the dark room. A bunk was built
into the wall opposite the cold hearth, and a
thin slab of wood was lying on top of a tree
stump beside it. Except for the bed, the tiny

table, and a crate set snugly against the back wall, the little room was empty.

"There's no one here," Caroline called to Eliza. "Come see for yourself."

Caroline gently pushed the door all the way open, and dust-flecked rays of light streamed into the shanty. A round-bellied mouse scampered over Caroline's bare feet and out the door. "Yikes!" she cried. "I hope he's the only critter here!"

"What's in that crate?" Eliza asked.

"I was wondering the very same thing," Caroline admitted. Turning to her dog, she smoothed the bristly hair on the side of his face and said, "Stay right here, Wolf, and warn us if anyone comes." Caroline then crossed the room in three quick steps and looked into the crate. The box was full of little birds and animals. "Come see this," she said excitedly, waving her sister into the room.

With a quick glance over her shoulder, Eliza hurried to Caroline's side. "All those little critters!" Eliza gasped. "Are they alive, Caroline?"

Caroline knelt down beside the box. A

brilliant blue jay, a ruby-red cardinal, and a clay-colored sparrow were perched together on one side, their claws mounted onto thick chunks of wood. Beside the birds, a ruddy brown squirrel sat with its paws pressed close together, ready to nibble at a nut. A gray-haired rabbit nestled at the squirrel's side, one furry ear raised, the other drooping over its shoulder. And in the opposite corner of the box, two frowning toads hunkered expectantly. Caroline rested her chin on the side of the crate and stared at their bulging eyes, half expecting the toads to hop out of the crate and greet her with a rumbling *ribbit.*

"None of these critters is breathing," Caroline said, waving her fingertips in front of the squirrel, "though they look as alive as any toads I've ever seen."

A sharp barking shattered the stillness in the little room. Wolf was yelping and snarling outside. "What is it?" Caroline called out in alarm as she bolted to the door. There, standing stock-still in front of Wolf, were two boys. The first boy was a whole head taller than the second, but both had mussed-up curly brown hair and deep-blue eyes. They looked like brothers and seemed to be a little bit older than she and Eliza. Both wore the same sort of dark trousers that Henry and Joseph always wore, and their bare chests were streaked with dirt and deeply tanned by the sun. Each boy was holding a dead raccoon by its bushy striped tail. The stiff animals' black button noses rocked slowly above the dirt.

"Quiet, hound! Who do you belong to?" The older boy was shouting above the barking. Then his eyes widened with surprise. Staring suspiciously at Caroline as she appeared in the doorway of the shanty, he cried, "Just what are you doing in our house? Get out of there, now!"

Wolf threw himself into the air and snapped his jaws at the angry boy. Caroline rushed to Wolf's side as his paws landed on the ground. "Hush now," she soothed the growling animal, patting his back. Then she turned back to the boys. "The door was open when we passed by, and we didn't do anything but look inside," she explained in as firm a voice as she could muster. "Besides, if this place belongs to you," she challenged, "then why is it in *our* forest?"

"This forest don't belong to nobody but God Almighty!" the older boy snapped. "Me and my brother here, we found this shanty. We're keeping it for ourselves."

"This forest belongs to my mother," Caroline countered. "You should find a house in your own forest!"

"Let's go," Eliza whimpered. She was standing behind Caroline, tugging at the corners of her apron. "I want to go home."

"In a minute, Eliza," Caroline promised. "Are those your birds and animals in there?" she asked, her voice softening.

"Every last one," the older boy snarled. "We found 'em. We stuffed and mounted 'em. You can't have them. Not one. So I say, go away!"

Wolf growled a warning and leaned toward the boy. "Hush, Wolf," Caroline repeated, her focus on the boy unwavering, her insides feeling braver every minute. "*I* say quit acting like the biggest toad in the puddle and be quiet!" she said. "I don't want your old stuffed animals. I thought they were fine to look at, is all, and was just about to tell you so. But now I've changed my mind, on account of your terrible manners."

The older boy looked startled. He opened his mouth to respond, but the younger boy spoke first. "See my bird?" he asked haltingly.

Caroline watched silently as he stepped around her and Wolf and walked into the hut, his raccoon swinging by his side. In a moment he was standing before her again, cradling a wide-eyed owl in his dirt-caked hands.

"You c-can hold it," he stammered, lifting the bird up to Caroline.

Gripping the corners of the wooden stick that held the owl, Caroline examined every inch of the stunning bird. Gleaming black pupils and golden eyes rimmed by snowy white feathers stared back at her, and a thick covering of brown, gray, and white feathers nearly hid the bird's pointed black beak. "It's the prettiest owl I ever saw," she breathed, stroking the bird's silky speckled coat. Handing it back to the little boy, she said, "Thank you for showing me."

"Come back." The boy spoke each word slowly, as he took the owl from Caroline. "To see the raccoon I'll make. Miles'll make one, too," he added. Then he disappeared into the shanty.

"Wally stuffs birds and toads better'n anybody," the older boy said proudly. Then he turned to Eliza. "You can come back if you want," he said grudgingly. "Bring her, too, so long as she doesn't say nothing about manners." Without so much as a backward glance at Caroline, the boy stomped off into the shanty and slammed the door tightly closed behind him.

"We're going to get in big trouble with Mother," Eliza worried as she reached for Caroline's hand and followed her back through the woods.

"I never met such strange folks," Caroline said. "Not ever."

"Where are you going?" Eliza pulled on Caroline's hand. "We have to go to the river to get Henry and Thomas."

"I forgot," Caroline said, turning in the opposite direction. "This way, Wolf."

Walking along in silence, the girls moved quickly through the glimmering forest, and soon they heard Henry's rollicking song floating along on the breeze. "There they are," Eliza said happily, as Henry appeared between the trees, a dripping Thomas straddled on his shoulders.

"Looky there, Thomas! A couple of strays to take home from the forest!" Henry joked as Wolf bounded up his side.

Eliza laughed. "Mother sent us to fetch you for dinner."

"Good!" Henry exclaimed. "I'm so hungry, I could eat a river full of trout and a barrel full of corn bread!"

"Me, too!" Thomas echoed.

"Then let's take the quickest trail home," Henry suggested.

"We won't get to show Henry the shanty," Eliza fretted as they stepped into the sun-drenched clearing.

"We'll show him another time," Caroline said.

"The hut out back in the woods?" Henry asked. He lifted Thomas off his shoulders and dropped him lightly to the ground.

"Have you seen it before?" Caroline asked.

"Passed it plenty of times. Even poked my head in once," Henry added. Picking up a big stick and swinging it at each tree trunk he passed, he continued, "Nothing in there but a bunk and a rickety old table. Joseph and I figured some settler built it to live in while he chopped timber and made a bigger house for him and his family. Seems the bigger house never got made."

"Is it on Mother's land?" Caroline asked.

"I don't know," Henry answered.

"We found it and went inside today, too!" Eliza told her brother.

"What'd you see?"

"Same as you," Caroline said quickly, giving Eliza a warning look.

"I'm hungry," Thomas said. "Let's go faster!"

"Race you to the door, weasel," Henry teased, and he bounded around stump after stump in pursuit of his little brother.

"Why can't we tell Henry about those boys and their box?" Eliza asked as soon as her brothers were out of earshot.

"Henry or Joseph might shoo them away like a bunch of pesky pigeons, especially if they're staying on Mother's land," Caroline answered. "Maybe those boys don't have any other place to live, so where will they go? We can't tell anybody about what we saw today, Eliza," Caroline declared. "Not till we find out more about those boys. Promise?"

Eliza nodded. "Promise."

"Where in heaven have you been?" Mother asked as Caroline and Eliza entered the house and breathed in the smoky aroma of fish and stewed vegetables.

"Finding the boys," Caroline answered, squeezing Eliza's fingers.

"Well, wash up and join the rest of us at the table," Mother said. "And next time, I expect you to find them a whole lot quicker."

"Yes, ma'am," Caroline said as she crossed to the washstand. Next time, she would be able to find the shanty in no time at all.

Peddler

"*Now come, all you young fellows that follow
    the sea—*
To me way, hey, blow the man down—
Oh please pay attention and listen to me;
Give me some time to blow the man down.

"*I will tell you a story, it's not very long—*
To me way, hey, blow the man down—
*It's about a young sailor bound home from
    Hong Kong;*
Give me some time to blow the man down."

Muffled one moment, booming the next, a jolly voice echoed through the clearing. Caroline peered over the knee-high stalks of corn rippling in the hot July breeze. "Who's that singing, do you suppose?" she called out to Eliza.

Eliza tugged a handful of weeds from the dirt beneath a pumpkin vine. "Is it Mr. Ben?" she asked excitedly, the broad leaves at her toes fluttering back to the ground like furry green fans.

Caroline shook her head. "It's a voice I've never heard before," she answered. "Let's go see who it is. Come on, Wolf," she said, patting the dog, who lay quietly beside her on the dusty ground.

Brushing the dirt from her hands, Caroline hurried out of the garden, Eliza and Wolf a step behind. From the southern tip of the clearing, a man was heading toward them. Two bulging leather pouches were slung over his shoulders, and the gray mule clomping along beside him carried another three.

117

"But for his hair, he looks just like one of the weeds in the garden," Caroline whispered as she looked at the man's green flannel shirt, green trousers, and bushy black hair. "I wonder what he wants."

Wolf crouched down, growling softly. "Maybe we should fetch Henry or Joseph," Eliza suggested nervously.

"He's some sort of traveler, I suspect. Or maybe he's lost his way," Caroline reasoned. "No sense in getting the boys 'fore we find out what he's come for."

Leading his donkey around a tangle of tree stumps, the man waved to the girls. "Good mornin' to you!" he exclaimed. "I'd heard some fellow Yankees had settled into the old cabin south of the river, and came to welcome you to our fair countryside! A pleasure to make your acquaintance, young ladies!" With a fancy flourish, the man bowed to the girls.

Caroline eyed the man suspiciously. She certainly wasn't a fellow, and she'd never heard the word "Yankee" before, so she didn't know whether to be pleased or troubled by such a description. Still, the man's kind brown eyes and wide smile were more than pleasant, so Caroline decided not to take offense. Strangers rarely wandered onto their land, and she always liked to speak to anyone who happened to pass through. "If you please, sir," she began, "we haven't yet made your acquaintance."

"William is the name, but most folks in these parts call me Zobey," the man responded.

"Such a funny name!" Eliza giggled.

"No stranger than the mule's, here." The man grinned. "His name's Ox!"

"Who'd ever name a donkey *that?*" Eliza asked.

"His owner, of course," he answered, shrugging his shoulders to shift the weight of his bulging sacks. "Might look like a donkey, but he's strong as an ox."

"Are you looking for a place to rest, Mr. Zobey?" Caroline asked.

"After I show you young ladies and the rest of your kin my wares, I might rest at that. Your mother and father, sisters and brothers—run and get them all. Grandfolks, too. I've brought

119

something for everyone."

"You're a tin peddler!" Caroline exclaimed. Once, years ago, before Father had voyaged out to sea, a tin peddler had visited Brookfield, his sacks stuffed with shiny pans, candlesticks, and boxes. Caroline still remembered the shiny tin lantern Mother had traded a whole sack of rags for, and how candlelight flickered daintily through the tiny holes that had been punched in the tin. Brookfield grew into a bustling town, though, and Mr. Porter opened his general store, filling the shelves with tinware. The tin peddler no longer had reason to visit, and he carried his goods elsewhere. Caroline hadn't seen him again.

"I'm a simple peddler is all," the man corrected, "though the donkey has a fine selection of tinware on his back, if tinware's what you're wanting. Where might I lay a blanket, miss?" he asked, looking around for a stumpless spot of earth. "I'll need plenty of room to set out my goods."

"There's room next to the woodpile," Caroline said. "I'll take you there. Eliza, run and tell Mother a peddler's come. Tell Martha, too. I'll get Joseph and Henry."

Urging his donkey along, Zobey followed Caroline and Wolf across the clearing to the far side of the house, where Henry and Joseph were splitting timber for the woodpile. "You can lay the blanket there, sir," she said, pointing to a wide patch of dry grass between the woodpile and the house.

"Fine!" The peddler paused. "Now what's your name, young lady?"

"Caroline, sir."

"Miss Caroline, how 'bout if I find something for you before your sisters and brothers arrive?" Zobey slid the leather sacks off his shoulders and dropped them lightly to the blanket. "Some buttons, perhaps, or thread for your sampler? A new doll? A hair ribbon, maybe?"

Caroline's eyes lit up. She hadn't had a new ribbon for her hair since Mother had made her a dress for the March frolic in Brookfield more than a year ago.

"A ribbon it is!" Zobey chuckled and tugged

the remaining sacks off the donkey's back.

"Would you prefer satin or lace?" he asked, rummaging through one of the smaller bundles.

"May I please see them all?" Caroline asked as he opened his hand. One by one, he placed the ribbons on his blanket: a blue satin ribbon and one made of frilly white lace, a yellow-dot calico ribbon and a green plaid, two ruby-red flannel ribbons and still another of soft black velvet.

"They're so pretty," Caroline said softly. She reached out toward the black velvet ribbon. "May I touch it, sir?" But before Zobey had a chance to speak, Caroline snatched back her fingers and cried out, "Oh! My hands are still dirty from the garden! I have to go wash them first. Could you wait just a minute, please?"

"Take it, child," the peddler said, handing her the velvet ribbon. "You won't be the first that's left a smudge or two of dirt on my wares. It brushes off clean."

Wiping her hands on her apron, Caroline took the ribbon and gently rubbed the velvety material between her fingertips. "I never felt anything so soft," she whispered.

"It'd sure look pretty tied 'round the bottom of your braid, Miss Caroline." Zobey stuck his arm into another sack and began rummaging around. "Ah, here it is," he said, pulling out a hairbrush with a silver-plated handle. "First you brush, then braid, then tie that ribbon into a pert little bow around the bottom of your braid."

"May I hold it, Mr. Zobey?" Caroline asked as she stared at the hairbrush, which flashed in the sunlight.

"It's as good as yours!" The peddler smiled as Caroline ran her fingers across the gray tips of the bristles. "Real boar hairs, those," he added.

Caroline brushed hard from her forehead to the top of her braid. The metal handle cooled her hand, and the boar bristles left her scalp tingling. How she wished she could brush her hair with a silver-plated brush with boar bristles every day, instead of the plain wooden brush she always used.

"Better find out what this fellow's wanting

for those things 'fore you take a liking to them, Caroline," Joseph suggested from behind.

"'Fore you know it, you'll be trading him Wolf for a hairbrush fine as that," Henry added knowingly.

Caroline's cheeks flushed a bright pink. The man was being so nice to her, she had forgotten that his treasures came with a price. "I'm sorry, sir," she said. "I don't have anything to give you for these fine things. Thank you for letting me hold them."

"Nonsense, child. Everyone has *something* to trade with a packman! Furs or ashes, even old mittens and coats! I can trade for most anything you can imagine, even your dried-out corn. It all depends on what you're willing to part with! And," the peddler added, turning to Joseph, "as for you young fellows, I've games and jackknives, pipes and boots for you to look at. So you ought to spend your next few minutes counting the numbers of furs and sacks of ash you have to trade, and less time scolding your little sister."

"What's all the fuss?" Mother's voice startled

Caroline. "What brings you here today, sir?"

"Mr. Zobey is a peddler, Mother," Caroline answered. "He's come to show us his wares."

"Yankee notions from a fellow Yankee, ma'am," the peddler informed Mother, winking. "It'll take me but a minute to unload these sacks and show you."

"So long as there's no price for looking, I'd like to see every last thing!" Mother said cheerfully.

"Me, too!" Martha and Eliza said together.

In no time at all, the blanket was covered with trinkets, tin cups and dippers, baskets and clocks, candlesticks and candleholders, shoes, boots, buttons, lace, and china-faced dolls with flouncy dresses.

"What are those?" Caroline asked, pointing to the middle of the blanket where a tin star, diamond, and heart glinted in the sun.

"They're cookie cutters," Mother answered.

"There are none that make a fancier cookie than these!" Zobey said.

"Look! That's me," Thomas cried. "In there!" Kneeling on one corner of the blanket, he was bending over a looking glass, making funny faces at himself.

"I like these little bitty men," Eliza said, holding up a small stand on which two painted wooden men hung from a slender post, one on top of the other.

"Give it a good flip of the wrist, child," Zobey said, laughing, "and you'll set them spinning like a circus wheel. Them whirligigs are as much fun as any toy I ever peddled."

"I could sure use one of these," Henry blurted out as he moved the silvery blade of a jackknife in and out of its base. "Think of the varmints we could skin with knives like this, Joseph."

"It's time we got each of you a jackknife," Mother agreed. "Perhaps next spring, when we're settled some."

"We've plenty of other knives to use till then," Joseph said. "They need to be sharpened is all."

"Not another word," Zobey said, reaching into a pouch that was tied around his calf.

"I've brought along my sharpening stone. Happy to do it for you, young man."

Joseph grinned and shook his head incredulously. "I'll go for the knives."

"Look, Caroline," Martha was saying, her voice awed. "Did you ever see such a pretty hairbrush?"

Spinning around from the doll she was examining, Caroline found her older sister picking up the silver-plated handle of the hairbrush she wanted, and she had to keep herself from shouting, "Put that down, Martha! I saw it first, and since when do you care about hairbrushes, anyway?" Biting her tongue, she said simply, "I saw it before. I liked it, too."

"Look how it shines!" Martha exclaimed. "I'd never grow tired of brushing my hair if I had such a thing to brush it with."

"Did you see all the ribbons he's brought?" Caroline said, trying to distract her sister. "I like the black velvet best. What about you?"

Still holding the hairbrush tightly in her hand, Martha looked at the colorful row of ribbons in the corner of the blanket. "I like the green one," she said, "and the lacy one, too."

"I'll take a paper of sewing pins, Mr. Zobey," Mother began. "A thimble, three needles, and five of your black buttons. And if you can pour me a small sampling of your sugar, I'd be most grateful."

"What will you take for the hairbrush, Mr. Zobey?" Martha asked boldly once Mother finished speaking. "I've a scarf I knitted that's very warm and pleasing to look at."

"My, but that hairbrush is special today," Zobey said with a meaningful glance at Caroline. "Have you decided not to trade for it, Miss Caroline?"

"I don't have anything but an old pair of mittens, and a few samplers that are mostly special to me," Caroline said. Her throat felt tight suddenly, and she could barely speak the words.

"Then the scarf it is!" Zobey said.

"I'll be right back, sir," Martha promised, handing Zobey the brush.

"You need your scarf more than you need a fancy hairbrush, young lady," Mother said firmly, catching hold of Martha's arm before she had a chance to leave.

"But I have time to knit another before the cold weather comes," Martha pleaded. "Please, Mother!"

"Then you ought to trade your shawl for enough new yarn to make another, since we won't have any wool to spin for some time," Mother said pointedly. "The little bit of yarn we have left is precious to us, and not to be traded for unnecessary things."

"Yes, ma'am," Martha said glumly.

"When you return next summer, Mr. Zobey," Mother requested, "please bring another hairbrush, just like this one. Martha will be certain to trade for it then."

"I'll bring two," the peddler promised, winking at Caroline.

Once Zobey finished sharpening knives, he packed up his belongings and turned to Mother. "Many thanks, ma'am," he said, as she handed him a sack full of calico and flannel scraps. "I'll be certain to return come springtime."

"Surely you'll stay for dinner," Mother said. "Buckwheat cakes and the last of our chipped beef and cellar vegetables. It isn't much but it's hearty, and I'd love to hear any news you may know."

The peddler readily accepted the invitation. As Caroline and Martha followed the others into the house, Martha whispered, "You wanted that brush, too, Caroline?"

"More than anything else I saw," Caroline admitted, "save the black velvet ribbon. I liked them both."

"You should have told me when I first picked it up," Martha said. Squeezing Caroline's arm lightly, she added, "I'm glad neither one of us got it, then," and hurried off to help Mother serve the meal.

Zobey was so full of news and stories, he barely had a chance to eat Mother's warm, filling meal. The war with Mexico had ended earlier in the year. President Polk's health was poor, and since he had refused to serve a second term, the Democrats were backing a fellow named Cass for president, while the

Whigs were behind General Zachary Taylor. "It'd knock me into a cocked hat if the Democrat gets elected, Taylor being a war hero and all," Zobey said.

"And Wisconsin?" Mother asked as she poured her guest a mug of steaming coffee. "Has it finally become a state?"

"May twenty-ninth, just past," the peddler answered. "To hear the townsfolk in Concord tell it, Kellogg threw quite a celebration. From all reports, his picnic and barn dance rivaled the Glorious Fourth. It's a wonder you haven't heard about it yet."

"Kellogg?" Mother asked.

"Austin Kellogg," Mr. Zobey answered. "Owns plenty of land in these parts and keeps buying more. He's the Justice of the Peace, and a Commissioner of Common Schools. Lives in the center of town with his wife, Laura, and their daughter, not three or four miles from here. Concord's first town meeting was held in his parlor the day before I first visited with his family. A fine man, not much more than thirty years old, I'd say. I expect he'll be governor of our new state 'fore long."

"I had no idea Concord was so settled," Mother said.

"Concord's barely a town yet, ma'am," Zobey said. "But there are plenty of settlers you can meet down by the crossroads. You ought to take a walk there someday soon."

"May I go, too?" Caroline asked. She hadn't imagined there'd be other folks living so close in all this wilderness. There might even be a school nearby, and maybe the daughter of this Mr. Kellogg could be her friend.

"We'll all go," Mother promised as Eliza, Thomas, and Martha opened their mouths to ask as well.

Long after every bite of food had been eaten, Zobey sat and told stories. When he finally gulped the last sip of his now-cold coffee, slapped his knees, and stood up to leave, Caroline couldn't bear to see the peddler go. She hadn't had so merry a dinner since Mr. Carpenter and Uncle Elisha had left months ago.

"Thank you again, ma'am, children," Zobey

said as he slung his leather sacks over his shoulder. "I expect next time I visit, there'll be some fresh-baked treats waiting." He pulled the star-shaped cookie cutter from his pocket and handed it to Mother.

Standing on the front stoop of the cabin with the rest of her family, Caroline watched the peddler and his donkey disappear into the woods, her mind full of ribbons and hairbrushes, and the town waiting for them down the road.

"Back to our chores, I'm afraid," Mother said, and shooed the children away. Caroline sighed and picked up a broom to sweep the floor.

Riverbank

D ay after day, the sun blazed. The forest stood motionless, and the browning leaves hung listlessly. The Quiners'
thin, shriveled corn hung from its stalks,
tiny white kernels sparsely filling the pockets
beneath the ears' hairy linings. Squash and
pumpkin plants lay limp on the parched earth,
leaves and vines fading to a sickly yellow-
brown. At each day's end, the sun slipped below the horizon, and its light disappeared. But
even the darkness couldn't dispel the stifling
heat.

Riverbank

As July gasped into August, Mother began praying for rain. "If it be Thy will, Lord, send us a shower to feed the plants and cool the air," she prayed one afternoon before dinner. "For this meal, we remain ever thankful. Amen."

"Amen," Caroline repeated. Sliding a spoon into her bowl of peas, she reached for her napkin and wiped it across her sweaty forehead and neck. Every thick, hot breath she took lodged in her throat.

"Will God answer your prayer and make it rain, Mother?" Eliza asked.

"We must keep praying," Mother answered. "He can't help but hear and answer."

Martha set her spoon down on the table and dropped her chin into her hands. "Do you think it was ever so hot before?"

"When I was almost your age, we suffered through a heat spell in Boston like none I've lived through since," Mother replied. "My father recorded forty-eight days without rain. Farmers lost their crops. Livestock collapsed and died in the heat. The land grew so hot and dry, we spent our days and nights living in fear of fire."

"Did anything burn?" Caroline asked.

"My family watched many friends and neighbors lose their homes and workshops to fire. Our house was mercifully spared, but your uncle Louis nearly died dragging a neighbor boy out of his burning parlor. Grandmother Tucker didn't leave his bedside for weeks, she was so afraid of losing him. Every morning and night she smoothed balm over his burned skin and changed his wraps. Louis was never the same after that summer." Mother's voice grew quiet as she finished speaking. "The fire burned away his boisterous laugh and easy manner. From that day on, he kept to himself."

Forks and spoons clanged against the pewter plates, but the children remained silent until Mother spoke again. "So you see," she said, her voice gently encouraging, "we have much to be thankful for. Even in all this heat."

"It has to rain again *sometime*!" Eliza blurted out.

"It certainly does, Eliza," Mother assured her. "Nevertheless, there are plenty of things to do. Even in all this heat."

"Like fishing, for one," Henry announced. "The river's so low and still, you can see straight to the bottom. Just this morning, there were whole schools of bluegill, pumpkinseed, and perch swimming around."

"No easier time to catch them," Joseph agreed.

Henry nodded, wiping crumbs of corn bread off his chin with the back of his hand. "If it's all right with you, Mother, I'll head upstream after dinner and catch us some supper."

"I've half a mind to go with you so I can wade in the cool water," Mother said, wiping her brow.

"Couldn't we all go, ma'am?" Caroline pleaded.

"And scare the fish away with your splashing feet?" Henry exclaimed indignantly.

"The water's anything but cool, Caroline," Joseph added. "In some spots it's warm as bean soup."

"But there are blackberries on the river-banks," Caroline countered. "They're falling off their branches, they're so ripe. Maybe we could pick some berries and then go into the river after Henry's caught his fish."

"That's a fine idea," Mother said. "Eliza, Martha, you can help Caroline. Then all of you can cool off in the water. No matter how warm it may be, it can't help but bring some relief from this heat."

"Yes, ma'am!" Eliza exclaimed.

"I want to go with Henry!" Thomas said, his words muffled by a mouthful of beets. "I can catch fish in my bucket!"

"It's easy enough for him to catch some perch and pumpkinseed," Joseph agreed. "Then I'll be able to finish the chores here."

"I'll stay too, and stir up some batter for blackberry cakes," Mother said. "Pick us as many berries as you can, girls! Enough to fill our bellies tonight, and still have plenty left for preserving."

"I could help you, Mother, if you'd like," Martha offered reluctantly. Caroline glanced at her sister. The wrinkle in Martha's brow and unhappy tilt of her lips filled Caroline with relief. Martha clearly wanted to pick berries and play in the river instead of helping Mother in the house. For the first time in months, since she had started acting so proper, Martha looked and sounded like herself again.

"Run along to the river, Martha," Mother said. "The more hands picking berries, the better."

"Yes, ma'am," Martha said, relief brightening her face as she dipped her spoon into her bowl again.

After dinner, Caroline and her sisters followed Henry and Thomas to the river. The glistening sun transformed the woodlands into a hazy golden arcade. Far above the trees, geese dipped and glided. Cicadas buzzed in gleeful crescendos. Winding along the forest's edge, the narrow river trickled peacefully from twist to turn.

"Do we have to pick berries this minute?" Eliza asked as they came upon the sparkling water. "Couldn't we go wading first, and then fill our baskets?"

"Henry doesn't want us scaring his fish," Martha said. "We'll have to walk much farther downstream if we want to go into the river first."

Dropping her baskets on the dry grasses below, Caroline shook her head. "I'm not walking one more step," she decided, lifting a corner of her apron and wiping her forehead and face. "Besides, if we pick the berries first, the water will feel even better after our baskets are full and we're hotter than ever."

"I think we should pick first, too," Martha agreed. "There's so many berries, it won't take any time at all."

Gazing at the purple-black brambles stretched along the banks of the river, Caroline chose a bush that was loaded with thick clusters of blackberries. Henry and Thomas passed beside her as she began pulling the sweet, juicy fruit from its tangled stems.

"I'm leaving my extra spear here by you, Caroline," Henry said, dropping one of the tall pointed sticks he was holding on the ground near her. "Don't let me forget to take it home again."

"I won't," Caroline promised, picking berries and listening to her brothers as they waded into the water.

"Where'm I supposed to find those pumpkins?" Thomas asked Henry.

"Pumpkin*seed*!" Henry answered, his voice low. "They're fish, not squash, runt. Little silvery things that dart through the water. Go look under those big rocks next to the riverbank." Tiptoeing across the boulders lying beneath the surface of the river, he crouched down and peered into the murky bottom. Caroline wondered what Henry was watching.

"I don't see any fish at all!" Thomas cried out, dangling the long strand of twine he was holding between his chubby fingers over the water.

"Shush! You'll scare them all away!" Henry scolded in a loud whisper. Balancing himself on a boulder with his fingertips, he patiently asked, "How are you s'posed to see anything,

Thomas, if you're looking into the sun? Turn around, and stay still. Any fish that sees your shadow moving over the water isn't going to fiddle around waiting for you to catch it."

Thomas did as he was told, then bent down to search for the wiggling shapes of perch and sunfish. "I still don't see any!" he complained, standing straight up and flicking drops of water off his nose.

"Then go look under those tree branches that are hanging over the river," Henry said. "The fish like hiding in all that shade. And stay low to the ground as you close in on the riverbank. Don't scare them away!"

Copying his older brother, Thomas crouched down and tottered from rock to rock until he was standing near the blackberry bushes on the river's edge. "I'm catching fish," he told his sisters. "Shhh." Then he climbed onto a rotted tree stump, dipped the little square of fatty mutton tied to the end of his twine into the water, and sat perfectly still. Caroline had just dropped another handful of berries into her basket when Thomas snatched the

twine out of the water and shrieked jubilantly,
"I got one! Look, I got one!"

"Good for you," Caroline said.

"I'm going to get some more," Thomas said
excitedly, pulling the tiny fish off the twine
and plopping it into his bucket.

Eliza stood on her tiptoes to look at her
little brother's catch. "How does Henry know
all those things about fishing?" she asked her
sisters.

"Father taught him how," Martha answered.

Caroline set down a brimming basket of berries. "Crooked Bone showed him, and Joseph
too," she said. "Remember Father's Indian
friend from Brookfield who—" she began;
then suddenly she stopped speaking. Pointing
at Henry, she lifted her finger to her lips, signaling her sisters to be quiet. "He's about to
catch one, I think," she whispered.

Holding her breath, Caroline watched as
Henry bent over and dipped his hands into
the water. Motionless, he waited. Then, in a
flash of arms and hands and fingers, he
scooped his cupped hands out of the water

and flipped a shimmering gold trout through the air. It landed with a thud only steps away from Caroline, Martha, and Eliza, and began to wriggle frantically on the earth beneath a leafy blackberry branch.

"That's some trout!" Eliza exclaimed.

Pointing to the flailing fish as her brother bounded out of the river, Caroline called out, "It fell over there!"

Henry picked up the trout and whacked its head against a rock. Tossing the dead fish into Thomas's pail, he tugged at Eliza's apron strings. "Plenty more to follow, I hope." Then, in a flash, he was in the middle of the river again, bent over the water, his arms immersed.

The sun had begun to descend through the trees when Thomas dropped his twine on top of the perch, sunfish, and trout that were stuffed into his pail, then struggled to lift it. "It's heavy!" he yelled. "There's no room for any more fish, Henry!"

"Quiet!" Henry scolded. "There's bound to be room for one more. At least!"

"See that, Eliza?" Martha asked as she

looked into her youngest sister's basket. "Thomas and Henry are all done fishing. I don't have a single space in my basket for one more berry, and Caroline's almost finished with her picking, too. But your basket's not even close to full," she chastised, her arms crossed disagreeably. "I'm hotter than a firefly in July! Now pay more attention to picking your berries, so we can go wading."

Eliza wrinkled her nose. "You *could* quit all your scolding and help me," she said sweetly. "I'm not as big as you, so that makes me a slower picker."

"I'll finish filling my basket and then help you, Eliza," Caroline offered, "if you promise to hurry. Go ahead, Martha. We'll be in the river in no time."

Martha stripped down to her petticoats and plunged into the river. Dashing to and fro, she roused the still river into a bubbly, swirling pool. "Come in!" she exclaimed gleefully, flinging her arms high above her head and sending a rainbow fan of droplets into the air.

"You're scaring all the fish," Henry grumbled. "Wade downstream till I'm finished."

Hopping across the riverbed, Martha called out, "Leave your pail there, Thomas, and come with me. Caroline and Eliza will find us downstream when they're finished. Is that all right with you, Caroline?"

Caroline waved Martha along. She was growing crosser and crosser as each stifling moment passed, and wishing she hadn't spent so much of her berry-picking time watching Henry teach Thomas how to fish. "Hurry now, Eliza," she urged. "There are so many berries here! We should have finished a long time ago."

"Jumping jackrabbits!" Henry's shriek echoed across the river.

Startled, Caroline squeezed her hands tight, crushing the berries she had just picked. "Oh, no!" she groaned, shaking the warm purple fruit and juice off her fingers.

"It's a northern!" Henry shouted.

"What's a northern?" Eliza asked.

"It's a big fish," Caroline explained. "Henry's going to try and spear it, I bet!"

146

Standing on the riverbank, Caroline and Eliza watched as Henry yanked his spear out of the riverbed and plunged it into the water again and again. After one especially harsh stab, his spear cracked and broke in half. "Dash it all!" he yelled. "I need my other spear, Caroline. Bring it to me, quick!"

Caroline looked all around her until she found Henry's spear lying beneath a blackberry bush. "It must have rolled under there when he dropped it," she said, retrieving the pointed stick. "Finish picking your berries, Eliza. I'll be right back."

Without a moment's hesitation, Caroline lifted her skirt above her knees and stepped into the warm water. The slippery, jagged rocks on the riverbed hurt her feet, but she paid them no mind. Eyes fixed on Henry, she crossed the river, wading deeper and deeper into the still water.

"Go slower," Henry said, his voice hushed. "The northern's just snaked by again. It's somewhere close."

Stepping cautiously, Caroline moved toward

Henry. Once she was close enough, she lifted his spear high above the water and handed it to him, pointed side first.

"Now stand still a minute," Henry whispered. "The less we move, the sooner we'll see the northern."

Caroline stood silently, watching a swarm of mosquitoes flitter above her head. Wiping her brow with the back of her sleeve, she wondered if slapping a mosquito once it landed on her bare skin would make enough noise to frighten away a northern. She was just about to ask Henry when something cold and slippery slithered against her leg.

"Something's here," she whispered, pointing to her legs.

"Don't move," Henry cautioned, trudging slowly through the water.

The muddy depths of the river closed in around Caroline's ankles, holding her firmly in place. She tried to remember everything her brothers had ever said about the big fish they called northerns, but all she could recall was that they had sharp teeth and were very

hard to catch. "Hurry, Henry," she whispered nervously.

The muscles in Henry's neck twitched as he moved along without speaking or looking at his sister. His blue eyes were steely and determined. As he stepped beside Caroline, he lifted his spear high above his head and stared down into the river. Caroline shut her eyes tight as Henry plunged the spear into the river with all his might.

"I just missed the varmint!" he shouted. His spear shuddered back and forth. Yanking the stick out of the riverbed, he wiped off the sweat pouring down his flushed face. "It'll be back soon, no doubt," he told Caroline. "Go help Eliza if you want."

"Good luck," Caroline said with a sigh of relief. The glassy surface of the river rippled gently outward, and the swarm of mosquitoes followed her as she walked slowly through the water. Caroline had taken only a few steps when a thick, slimy creature brushed past her legs again. "It's back," she called out to Henry, trying not to move. "Over here."

"Stand still," Henry directed. Seconds later, he was standing beside his sister once again, his spear poised high above his head.

The hot sun beat down on Caroline as she waited for the northern to reappear. When she finally glimpsed a long, dark figure gliding through the water behind her, she waved her hands furiously, signaling Henry. Henry hurled his spear into the river.

"The blasted fish must know I'm after him!" Henry cursed as the northern flashed away. Exasperated, he jerked the spear out of the riverbed once more.

"I'm leaving before it comes back," Caroline said, and she was running across the river before her brother could say another word.

Eliza had filled her basket with berries and was skipping along the riverbank when Caroline caught up to her.

"Did Henry get his fish?" Eliza asked.

"Not yet," Caroline answered, shuddering as she remembered the slimy feel of the fish. "Let's get as far away from this part of the river as we can. I don't care how many more berries I still have to pick."

Together Caroline and Eliza ran downstream until they found Thomas sliding into the river from a rickety old bridge that was made of logs.

Martha waved to her sisters. She was sitting at the edge of the bridge, and was kicking her legs. Her soaked petticoats clung to her thin frame, and her dripping hair clumped all about her head. "Hurry!" she cried happily.

"I can't wait to get in," Eliza exclaimed as she pulled her dress up over her head.

"Me, too," Caroline agreed, glancing at the river. Was the frothy, sparkling water beneath the bridge hiding more northerns? Deciding she was too hot to worry about it, Caroline undressed down to her petticoats and ran after Eliza.

The sun dallied behind the forest as the girls and Thomas splashed in the river. They teetered and hopped across the log bridge, and gobbled up handfuls of berries along the banks on the far side of the river. Finally, they pulled on their clothes and headed upstream to retrieve their baskets and pails.

"That sure was fun!" Martha sang out.

"I'm glad you didn't stay home," Caroline said. "It's always more fun when you come with us."

"For me, too!" Martha winked at Caroline, who smiled back.

Henry was still standing in the middle of the river when they arrived, gripping his spear and staring into the water.

"We're back," Martha called out, lifting her baskets of berries.

Defeated, Henry stomped across the river. "That northern whupped me good," he said, climbing out of the water. Angrily, he pitched his spear over his sisters' heads, and it sailed into the forest. "Give me the pail, Thomas. It's high time we get back for supper."

As they walked back home through the quiet woods, Caroline couldn't help but feel sorry for Henry. She wished he had speared his big fish. Still, their baskets were overflowing with juicy ripe berries, and their pails were full of little fish that would surely taste every bit as good as one big one. The warm water had been more than refreshing in the stifling heat. And best of all, Martha was acting like Martha again.

Storm

Caroline lugged a pail of water across the clearing. Wolf softly panted as he trotted along beside her. "Where should I put this?" she called out to Joseph.

"Over here." Joseph beckoned with one hand from the row of potato plants where he was kneeling. Hurriedly, he dug up a circle of dirt around the stem of one leafy plant and moved on to the next.

Setting the pail down beside her brother, Caroline pulled her skirt away from the warm water sloshing over the sides. "What are you doing?" she asked, pushing blowing wisps of hair out of her eyes.

"I'm digging these wells around the bottoms of the plants so the rainwater can collect in them," Joseph answered. "There are some mighty fierce clouds up there. They're certain to bring us rain before suppertime."

Caroline gazed at the dark, bloated underbellies of the clouds swiftly crossing the sky. She wondered if they were carrying any rain. In the two long weeks since she had picked berries along the riverbank, many ominous clouds had floated by, but not a single drop of rain had fallen. The Quiners had spent their evenings carting buckets of water from the river to feed the withering vegetables in their garden. Caroline's arms ached, her fingers and hands were blistered, and she was beginning to think it might never rain again.

"What makes you so sure it's going to rain?" she asked, not believing her brother.

"I can smell it coming," Joseph said. "You can stop bringing water from the river now,

Caroline. No need to go to all that trouble, since the rain will do the watering for you."

Caroline had never smelled rain coming before. Inhaling the moist, musky scent of the air, she studied the brooding sky again. Even if those clouds weren't planning to rain, they were giving her a break from more long hot trips to the river, and she was grateful. "Should I tell Martha and Henry to stop now too?" she asked her brother.

Joseph shook his head. "I already told them. They're over in the corn patch, digging more wells." Glancing at the sky, he said, "We'll have to work fast, because we don't have much time left. Leave that water here and go help them finish. I want a well dug around every plant in the garden before the rains come."

"I had to leave one of my buckets by the river, Joseph, because I couldn't carry two back at the same time," Caroline explained. "I'll go for it quick, and then I'll help you finish your digging."

"Best to leave it there, and get it when the

rain stops," Joseph warned. "The winds are picking up, and it's getting darker by the minute. You might not make it home before the storm."

"But I have to get it!" Caroline exclaimed. "It's that really big pail Henry used to feed Hog with when we lived in Brookfield. He told me never to take it anyplace where I might lose it, since we're certain to get another hog soon, and he'll need it for feeding again."

"So why'd you take it in the first place?"

"It has an old shirtsleeve wrapped around its handle," Caroline admitted. "My hands were hurting, and that bucket doesn't dig into my fingers like the other pails."

"If I had the time, I'd get it for you, Caroline," Joseph said. "But digging these wells is more important than anything right now. Even Henry's bucket. Go help him and Martha."

Caroline walked toward the corn patch, Wolf following closely. She looked back at Joseph. He was working intently, paying no attention to anything but the wells he was digging around the potato plants. "Come on, Wolf," she said. "We'll go get Henry's bucket and be back before anyone misses us."

Hot, dusty air swirled about Caroline and Wolf as they hurried through the forest. The trees bent this way and that, branches twisting in protest as the wind flung their browning leaves all about. Squirrels hid, and sparrows swallowed their songs. The wind howling in her ears, Caroline ran out of the woods and rushed to the spot where she'd left Henry's pail.

Even though the river held much less water than usual, it churned and sputtered raucously. "The river's almost as mad as the sky!" Caroline exclaimed. Grabbing the pail by its cloth-covered handle, Caroline started on the path for home. "We better go right home, Wolf. The water wasn't nearly so unsettled when I was here before. Joseph must be right about a storm coming."

Splat. A fat raindrop struck Caroline's cheek as she dashed back into the forest, Wolf at her heels. *Splat. Splat.* Wiping the drops from her cheeks and eyes, she cried, "The rain's here, Wolf! We have to go faster!"

Wolf barked loudly and ran after Caroline, through piles of leaves and over jutting tree roots. Below the green-black, frenzied skies, all but a trace of daylight disappeared from the forest, and the woods surrendered abruptly to the wind's fury and the whipping rain.

Ducking her head against the sudden downpour, Caroline ran even faster. Within moments, her dress and apron were soaked and clinging to her body. She had to slow down. "Oh, why did I go back for that pail?" she muttered between clenched teeth. "I can't even see where we're going."

Caroline plodded on in the dim light, her stomach flipping over and over. Streaks of lightning bolted above, bathing the forest in flashes of bright white light, and she squinted to see far ahead. Unable to find her path, Caroline trudged across the glistening forest floor, refusing to stop.

Crack! A splintering bough snapped, and a long, jagged limb crashed through the trees and landed behind Caroline. She leaped out of the way as Wolf yelped, then bounded over the fallen tree limb and its protruding branches. "Wolf!" Caroline cried, dropping her bucket and rushing to the dog.

Caroline pulled Wolf to her and hugged him for a moment before searching through his fur for any wounds. "That branch could have . . ." she began, then quickly stopped when she discovered a bright-red scrape across his hind leg. "It's just a little scratch," she said soothingly, stroking the dog's side. "I'll see to it as soon as we get home. If we can find our way there," she added, retrieving the bucket.

Pounding raindrops stung Caroline's face and blurred her vision as she and Wolf moved slowly forward. Trying to find something familiar to lead them home, she searched for the elm tree with the two round knotholes where woodpeckers pecked, one above the other, and the maple tree that leaned so far to one side, it was certain to topple in all this wind. But the trees before her blended into a solid black tangle of wet limbs and branches. Even the path she had followed to the river had disappeared beneath a soggy blanket of leaves and twigs.

The farther Caroline journeyed, the more unfamiliar the woods became. Swallowing the panic rising inside, she finally stopped walking. "It's no use, Wolf," she shouted above the wind. "Let's wait under that fir tree until the storm stops. Joseph will figure out where we are. He'll find us."

Caroline led her dog to a stately fir tree up ahead and crawled beneath its fragrant branches. The dirt was damp beneath her legs, and the tree swayed in the wind. But its soft, dense boughs shielded her from the rain and snapping limbs that plunged to the ground around her. "We'll be safe here," Caroline told Wolf as she pulled him beneath the tree with her.

Humming every song she could remember, Caroline waited beneath the fir tree. She counted the leaves that skipped by in front of her, and recited all the Bible verses she knew. But the storm raged on with no sign of stopping. Caroline got colder and colder, and more and more scared.

"Come out from there!" a boy's voice suddenly shouted.

Caroline peered under the fir boughs and discovered two bare feet. Wiping her face with her dirt-smudged sleeve, she exclaimed, "Joseph! You've found us," grabbed hold of Henry's bucket, and crawled out from under her fir-branch shelter.

Barking madly, Wolf leaped in front of Caroline. "Down, Wolf!" she cried as she scrambled to her feet and grabbed hold of the dog. "It's just Joseph!"

Wolf growled menacingly as Caroline looked up for her brother. But Joseph wasn't there. Standing before her was Miles, the boy she'd seen by the shanty in the woods. His brown hair was plastered about his forehead, and his bare, rain-streaked chest had leaves stuck all over it.

"Why are you sitting under that tree?" the boy yelled above the shrieking wind.

"I got lost going home, and I was waiting for my brother to find me!" Caroline yelled back as she blinked away the pelting rain. "I can't see the path anymore. Can you please tell me how to get to my house?"

"What's it look like?"

"It's a cabin in the middle of a clearing. If you take me to your shanty, I can find my way from there, I think."

"I'll save your hide, long as we both agree it's *my* shanty."

Biting her tongue, Caroline called, "Come along, Wolf," and followed the boy slowly through the forest, ducking her head behind his bare back as they walked into the wind.

In a flash of lightning that lit up the forest, Caroline saw the boys' tiny shack in the distance. Her heart leaped, for she knew the way home now. "Where's Wally?" she shouted at Miles's back.

"He's inside," Miles shouted over his shoulder, "like most anybody in these parts what's got a brain in his head."

Flushed with anger, Caroline took a deep,

calming breath. Then she asked, "Is he all alone?"

"Small as he is, he's much better at being left alone than you are, from the looks of it."

As furious now as the storm raging around her, Caroline dropped her pail and yanked on Miles's arm, spinning him around to face her. "You are the meanest boy I ever met," she shouted. "I'd rather be lost in this forest *forever* than have the likes of *you* help me!" Turning to her dog, she commanded, "Follow me, Wolf. We're going home."

Caroline ran off through the forest, Wolf barking at her heels. She passed the shanty, the knotty elm, and the leaning maple that glistened and shook in the pounding rain. As she raced into the clearing, the rain stung her skin and the wind whipped at her so harshly, it nearly knocked her off her feet. Bowing her head, Caroline flew forward until she caught sight of the dim yellow light glowing behind the hide-covered windows in the cabin ahead.

When she finally arrived at the door of her little house, Caroline could barely muster the strength to push it open. Leaning against the hard wood, she kicked at the door, and fell into Henry the moment he opened it.

"She's here!" Henry shouted.

"It's Caroline!" Martha and Eliza exclaimed.

"Goodness glory, Caroline!" Mother rushed to the door and cradled her daughter in her arms. "What were you thinking, going off to the river with a storm like this brewing?" she asked, tears of relief filling her eyes. "You might have been killed, child!"

Breathless and shaking, Caroline hid her face in Mother's apron. "I didn't think it would come so fast," she said, her teeth chattering. "And I wanted to save Henry's bucket. Oh!" Caroline gasped as she remembered that after all that, she had left the bucket by Miles's shanty.

"Never mind the bucket. Let's get these clothes off and sit you in front of the fire," Mother said. "It'll be a miracle if you don't take fever, drenched and shaking with cold as you are."

"Should I go for Joseph?" Henry asked.

"No," Mother said quickly. "He'll come back soon enough, and I won't have another child of mine out in this storm." Taking Caroline by the shoulders, she began leading her toward the bedroom as they heard three loud knocks at the door. "Who could be out in this weather?" Mother exclaimed incredulously. "Open the door, Henry."

Henry opened the door. Miles was standing there in a flurry of rain and wind, a heavy wooden bucket dangling from his outstretched hand. "Give this to your sister," he shouted at Henry as he handed him the bucket. "And tell her it was right smart of her to find shelter like she did." Without another word, Miles turned and walked off into the tempest.

"Who was that?" Henry asked after he shut the door against the wind.

"A boy who lives in the woods," Caroline answered. "Not such a mean boy, after all."

"You've met him before?" Mother asked.

"Just once," Caroline admitted. "His name is Miles. He has a little brother he calls Wally."

"I'd like to hear more about these boys after

you've eaten a hot meal and rested some," Mother said.

"Yes, ma'am," Caroline promised.

Soon after she was snug in her warm flannel underclothes and warming herself beside the blazing fire, Joseph returned. Soaked to the skin, he knelt in front of his sister and chided her. "You'll listen to me from now on, no matter what," he warned. Then his voice became gentle. "Mostly, I wish I'd have gone for that silly bucket, Caroline. We never had a hope of finishing those wells before the storm hit. Lucky for us, there's enough rain falling to soak the plants good."

"Looks like we'll have to get ourselves a hog, now," Henry said as Mother placed a steaming bowl of stew in front of Caroline. "An extra big hog that's worthy of such an important bucket!"

Digging into her stew, Caroline fervently promised, "I won't ever take it again!"

Making Plans

For two long days and nights, the wind whipped and roared outside the cabin. Rain poured from raging skies. On the dawn of the third day, sunlight burst through the stocky white clouds that capped the clearing, and the wind was replaced with a gentle breeze.

"I reckon the storm's ended for good," Henry announced as he entered the house with an armful of logs and piled them into the iron stove. "You should see the clearing, though. Looks more like a river, there's so many pools of water floating on it. The rain near filled a bucket I left by the woodpile, and soaked the ground into a marshland worse than we had out back of our house in Brookfield."

"And the garden?" Mother set her wooden spoon into her mixing bowl and looked at Henry.

Setting the plates about the table, Caroline watched her brother shake his head. He looked somber. "Joseph's tending to the garden while I bring in the wood," he said, hedging.

"For goodness' sakes," Mother said impatiently, beating the johnnycake batter into a creamy puff. "You must have seen *something*."

"Well, I didn't see too many cornstalks that were still standing."

Mother stopped her beating for a moment. "Call your brother, Henry-O, and tell him it's near time to eat. From the sound of it, we will have plenty of work to do in the garden this morning."

Joseph finally arrived, washed up, and sat down at the table. Martha piled his plate with food, and Mother said grace. With all the clanging of forks against plates and tin cups on the table that followed, only Caroline noticed that her older brother didn't say a word or swallow a single bite of his breakfast.

After breakfast, the family crossed the swamplike clearing, water and mud oozing above their ankles with each step. Caroline didn't like the cold clammy feel of the mud between her toes, and kept trying to kick it off as she walked.

Mother arrived at the garden first. She was surveying the damage, one hand covering her mouth, when Caroline stepped up beside her. "Oh no," Caroline said softly, her heart pounding in her ears as she looked out over the land. The droopy black stems and crumpled leaves of the pea plants were plastered on the dirt. Stalks of windblown corn were hunched over on their sides, many broken in half. Half-grown, yellowing pumpkins were sheared off their vines and lying in puddles of water.

"Where'd our garden go?" Thomas asked.

"Looks to me like somebody picked the

whole thing up by its roots and dropped it on top of itself," Henry said.

"I think we'll still be able to harvest some of the plants," Joseph told Mother. "A few of the pumpkins I saw this morning had fallen off their vines. But we can still use them, even if they won't grow anymore. We just have to quick get them off the ground before they soften in all that water and spoil."

Mother lifted a limp pile of cornstalks from the wet earth and ran her fingers across the soggy leaves, shaking her head in disbelief. "The wind pulled them right out of the ground," she said, her voice grave. "First the never-ending heat and drought. Then a whole summer's worth of rain falls in two days and ruins the crops. It doesn't seem possible."

Perplexed, Caroline said, "But you always say, 'Whatever a man soweth, so shall he reap.' How can anything ruin all our vegetables, when we worked so hard to make them grow?"

"'Every man shall bear his own burden,'" Mother said, repeating it to herself as she stared across the field. "We will bear this burden, too, Caroline, as we have many others."

"Yes, ma'am," Caroline said, not really understanding.

"Mr. Ben told us that when you clear timber, the first seeds you sink into that land won't grow into regular crops," Henry said. "He told me and Joseph we should work hard tending the crops, but not be disappointed if we only harvest half of what we planted."

"We'll salvage what we can," Mother said. "The carrots and turnips, and some of the potatoes and onions, may have survived underground."

Angrily, Joseph ripped a handful of cornstalks from the dark earth and tossed them across the field. "Not enough to last us through the winter, I can tell you that!"

"We'll make do," Mother said sternly. "We always have before. Stay here, children, and gather everything you can. I'll go back to the cabin and see to dinner."

Caroline watched Mother hurry off to the house, her head bowed. She was struck by how calmly Mother took the worst of news, and wondered if Mother felt as scared inside as she did. Even if Mother was scared, she didn't show it, and Caroline was thankful. Nothing was worse than seeing Mother cry.

"Let's get to work," Henry exclaimed. "I say we race! The one who fills his basket fastest and fullest wins!"

"How'm I supposed to know what to fill my basket with?" Thomas asked.

"Open every ear of corn you can find," Joseph instructed. "If you see any kernels inside, wrap them back up and put them in a bucket for keeping. Henry, you work alongside Thomas, and help him if he needs it. Make certain he doesn't miss a single ear."

"Or a single nose," Henry teased, "or a single eyeball, or a single—"

Joseph interrupted his brother. "This is no time for jokes. I'll help you, too, soon as I fetch pails for everyone. Eliza, Caroline, go over and dig through the peas, peppers, and squash. Martha, see to the pumpkins."

Caroline and Eliza trudged across the garden,

sinking through pools of water into the cool, sticky mud. "I don't even see any vegetables," Eliza said, her voice rising in fear. "What will we eat if we can't find any vegetables?"

"Don't be so grum, Eliza," Caroline said, pretending to be as calm as her mother. "They're just underwater, or hiding beneath the dirt." Kicking a stringy black vine off her foot, she said, "Look, here's a row of peppers. Let's start here."

Silently, Caroline and Eliza picked over the yellow and orange peppers that were scattered about the field. Flicking the mud off the skinny, crinkled vegetables, they dried them with their aprons and dropped them into the bucket Joseph had left at the edge of the garden.

"All sorts of these little green peppers that are no bigger than a button are lying around." Eliza showed Caroline a handful she had collected. "Should we keep them, too?"

"Mother could use them in her stews," Caroline decided. "Best to put them in the bucket."

Once they finished combing through the peppers, Caroline and Eliza moved on to the peas. Snapped in half or torn out by their roots, the plants lay helpless, shiny crescent pods still hanging from their branches. Bending down, Caroline ran her fingertips across the smooth, rubbery sheaths, hoping to feel a bumpy line of peas beneath their skin. But the pods felt hollow, so Caroline pulled some open. Instead of peas, in pod after pod she discovered rows of pale-green ovals that were even tinier than baby teeth. "The peas never started growing at all." She sighed. "Still, Mother might be able to cook the pods."

Long past dinnertime, Caroline and her brothers and sisters picked through their almost lifeless garden, filling their buckets with any food they could find.

"Let's see who's the winner," Henry called out, once they had all carried their pails to the side of the cabin. "Just this once, I hope it isn't me."

Henry peered inside each bucket. "Not one of us filled more than half," he said glumly.

"And most of what's in there doesn't look the least bit eatable. We can't show Mother these buckets, nohow. Not till we go back out there and look for more food."

"There isn't any more to find," Joseph said. "No, we'll have to go inside now and tell Mother so she can make a plan. We don't have a hog to slaughter, or vegetables to store for the winter. And we can't live on what Henry and me hunt in the forest. We have to figure some other way to get money or food. Mother will know what to do."

"I want to go inside and eat!" Thomas whined.

"Shush," Eliza said. "This is more important than your eating."

Caroline spoke up. "Why don't we make a plan first ourselves? Then when we go inside to tell Mother about the vegetables, she won't feel so bad, because we'll already have figured out what to do."

"That's the best idea," Martha agreed.

"I'm hungry!" Thomas repeated.

"Shhhh!" the other five children said.

"I could sew little things for somebody," Caroline thought aloud, "or do their mending. I could clean houses, or take care of somebody who's sick. I could even help some with cooking, though I'm not much good at it yet."

"We could sell things," Martha said, her eyes brightening. "We could sell some of the carpet rag I sewed, or the mittens and scarves I knitted."

"Mother won't hear of us selling our mittens and scarves," Caroline reminded her sister.

"I can chop wood," Joseph said, "take care of someone's animals and clean their barn. I could even help build chairs and benches and other such things if I had the chance."

"We could offer to help some farmer take in his crop," Henry suggested. "But only if he'll give us some of the harvest."

"It's not likely that anybody in these parts will have much of a crop left," Joseph reasoned. "We could go back to Brookfield, though, and help any number of folks. The storm may have passed right by there."

"I could go too!" Martha cried. "I'll sure

get more money for things I sew if I sell them to folks who know me!"

"If we leave in the next few weeks, we'll get to Brookfield right about the same time as the passenger pigeons," Henry said. "Just think how much money we made from all the birds we trapped and sold last year, Joseph. Why not do it again?"

"We could probably do it right here in Concord," Joseph quickly agreed. "We just have to find out who's likely to buy them and ship them off to Madison or Milwaukee."

"Let's go tell Mother!" Caroline cried.

Chattering excitedly, the children bounded into the cabin and hurried to the table that Mother had finished setting long ago. "My, but that's a boisterous bunch!" She greeted them pleasantly, though her face was pale.

Once the family was seated around the table, Caroline looked from Joseph to Henry to Martha, wondering who would speak first. Eliza surprised them all.

"We didn't pick hardly any good vege-tables, since there weren't many to pick," she informed Mother. "But that shouldn't make you one little bit sad, because everybody has a plan. Everybody but me and Thomas, that is. Maybe you could help us think of one."

Swallowing a small bite of bread, Mother reached for her napkin on her lap and wiped her lips. "What plans are you speaking about, Eliza?"

In a jumble of words and exclamations, Caroline, Martha, Henry, and Joseph told Mother all the plans they had to make money. By the time they finished, Mother was beaming proudly at her children.

"It seems we've all been making plans," she said. "I've considered a few myself. I owned my own dress shop in Boston for years, for goodness' sakes. Why couldn't I clothe the town of Concord, as well?"

Caroline clapped. "We could help you cut all the cloth, and even hem some of the dresses, if you like."

Mother nodded. "You see, children, one of our plans, or maybe even two, is certain to work. Months ago, the peddler told us there were plenty of settlers in our new town. It's high time we sought them out. My mother always said, 'Be not forgetful to entertain strangers, Charlotte, for thereby some have entertained angels unawares.' We haven't yet met our angel. Once we go to town, perhaps we will."

"Can we go tomorrow?" Martha asked, clasping her hands together excitedly.

Shaking her head, Mother replied, "It'll take a few days' time to get ready for such a trip. None of us has worn our Sunday best in more than a year, and there's no doubt in my mind that every one of your dresses and trousers will need some stretching and mending. You've all been growing faster than I can keep up with, I'm afraid."

Caroline tried hard to recall the last time she had dressed in anything other than a faded, worn everyday dress. "Mrs. Stoddard's house," she exclaimed, remembering the exciting Maple Frolic they had attended in their neighbor's fine house. "We could wear the red plaid dresses you made us for Mrs. Stoddard's frolic!"

"We'll take them out tomorrow and see if they still fit," Mother promised. "Now eat your dinner, all of you. We've plenty of planning and working to do before we make our first trip to town."

Good Fortune

Shaking her head, Mother turned Caroline around slowly and studied her red plaid dress. "Short of adding several inches of cloth to your shoulders, sleeves, and hem, I can't imagine how we're ever going to make this dress fit," she said.

"Oh no, Mother, I can wear it just fine. I know I can," Caroline insisted. Tugging at the lace that fell halfway between her elbows and wrists, she scrunched her shoulders to make her arms look shorter. "Even if it's a little bit short, this dress will still be prettier than my everyday dress."

"You could barely get it over your head," Mother reminded her. "It's a wonder you didn't burst the seams when you pulled it on."

Looking across the tiny room at her sisters, Caroline complained, "But Martha's dress still fits her almost, and Eliza's is just a little bit small. I can't be the only one who goes to town in my same old everyday dress!"

"You've grown more than your sisters have this past year," Mother said gently. "I'm sorry, Caroline, but I simply don't have the cloth I need to make your dress the right size. I used it all when I made these three dresses last year."

Caroline was quiet for a moment, trying to think of how Mother could fix her plaid dress. "I have an idea," she suggested. "You could take the ribbons you made us, and use them for your extra cloth. They match our dresses perfectly, and between me and Eliza and Martha we have three of them."

Pulling her own sleeves down closer to her

wrists, Eliza looked at her sister sympatheti-
cally. "She could use my ribbon, Mother."

"Mine, too," Martha agreed.

"That would give me enough cloth to
lengthen your sleeves, Caroline," Mother said.
Pulling pins out from between her lips, she
jabbed them into her pincushion. "But your
shoulders will still be too tight, the sides of
your dress will be too narrow, and your hem
will be at least three inches too short. Wearing
this dress is simply not possible, and that's the
last I want to hear about it. Take your dresses
off now, girls, and give them to me. If we're
to get to town by week's end, I need to begin
mending today."

Caroline knew that tone in Mother's voice;
it meant no arguing. Sadly she glanced down
at her skirt, unable to look at her sisters. She
knew they'd be feeling sorry for her, and that
was almost as bad as having to wear her everyday dress to town. Slowly she lifted her dress's
delicate lace hem to her waist, and wiggled
the tight-fitting bodice up to her neck. Bending
her arms, she then tried to pull the dress over

her head. She moved from side to side and shrugged her shoulders up and down, but it was no use. She couldn't straighten her arms again. The too-tight dress was stuck on her head.

"Hold still," Mother ordered her squirming daughter. "If you pull any harder, you'll tear the cloth and Eliza won't be able to wear that dress when she's bigger."

For one wicked moment, Caroline longed to yank the dress right over her head and rip every seam. Never, never would she go to town wearing the same old brown dress she wore to clear the land, dig in the garden, tend the chickens, and carry sloshing water in splintery buckets. She kept still until Mother was ready to help her, and decided that she simply wouldn't go to town at all.

"Now, lift your arms up," Mother instructed, "and I'll pull the dress over your head. There." She sighed, looking over the garment with a critical eye as soon as it was in her hands. "No harm done." Turning back to Caroline, Mother hugged her tightly. "Don't you worry,"

186

she said. "I'll fix your everyday dress up as pretty as I can. It will look just like your Sunday best."

"I don't see why Caroline can't wear the blue church dress you made me when I was her age," Martha said as she handed her dress to Mother. "I bet it will fit her just fine."

Caroline took a breath so fast, she started to hiccup. Two years ago, she had enviously watched Mother cut and sew one of her own lovely blue dresses into a church dress for Martha. It was the softest, richest dress that Caroline had ever seen, and she had been certain that her boisterous older sister would stain or tear the dress before she ever had a chance to wear it. But Martha got into all sorts of trouble the day she wore her blue dress to church, and had actually worn it only a few times. Caroline knew the dress was as good as new. The thought of wearing it now left her all tingly with excitement.

"Oh, Mother," Caroline cried, clasping her hands together, "that's a perfect idea! Please may I wear Martha's dress?"

"It *is* a perfect idea!" Mother agreed. "I wish I had thought of it myself and saved you all this fretting. Wait here while I find it. It's in the trunk we've stored in the loft, I believe."

The moment Mother stepped out of the room, Caroline threw her arms around her sister, hugging her tight. "Thank you," she breathed, her face glowing.

"Don't thank me," Martha said. "You always liked that dress better than I did, anyway. It always reminded me of those hateful girls and the terrible things they said to me." She shuddered, remembering. "I wish I could forget that day forever."

Mother was suddenly in the doorway, holding the blue dress against her. It was as exquisite as Caroline remembered. The pale-blue fabric shimmered against Mother's own dark gray dress, and fold after fold of material floated softly down to her ankles. Closing her eyes, Caroline smiled blissfully as Mother slipped the silky, cool dress over her and tied the bow in the middle of her back.

"I'm so pleased that I never shortened this dress for you, Martha." Mother tugged gently on the hem to straighten it. "It would have been too short for Caroline, otherwise."

"Does it fit?" Caroline asked. "Please say it fits!"

"It needs a small tuck or two, here at the waist," Mother said, sounding surprised. "But other than that, it's almost as if I made it for you."

Fanning out the folds of her skirt, Caroline inspected the dress. To her delight, she couldn't find a smudge on it. "I'll keep it extra clean for you, Eliza," she promised. "Just like Martha did for me."

Martha rolled her eyes. "I didn't do it on purpose. I never cared much for dresses back then," she admitted, "no matter how pretty."

"How soon till we can go to town?" Caroline asked, as Mother slid the dress off her.

"Now that we've found you all something to wear, we should be ready to go right off the reel," Mother replied. "Two days' time, good Lord and good weather willing."

Caroline grabbed her sisters' hands. Together they whirled about the little room, spinning in a circle and singing:

"A pretty fair maid all in a garden,
A sailor boy came passing by;
He stepped aside and thus addressed her,
Saying, 'Pretty fair maid, won't you be
my bride?'"

Two days later, the Quiners set out for town, long hair braided and bowed, cowlicks tamed with bear grease; dresses, shirts, and trousers clean, crisp, and neat.

The cool morning air hinted of the autumn to come. All about the woods lay the hollow, empty shells of once-boisterous cicadas, and high above the trees, flapping flocks of squabbling geese planned their long journey south.

"Leaves are 'bout to fall," Joseph said, as he led the family southward to the territorial road.

"We can't hope for them to be more than brown this year with such little rainfall, I'm afraid," Mother noted.

"How soon till we get there?" Caroline
asked. Savoring the soft swish of her dress as
it swayed against her, she hoped they had a
ways to walk.

"I imagine it's no more than two miles as
the crow flies," Mother answered.

"What does the town look like?" Martha
asked.

"I don't rightly know," Mother admitted.
"When Uncle Elisha and I came to buy our
land, we never traveled through town. We
were eager to return to Brookfield as soon as
possible."

"Will there be a general store?" Eliza
wondered.

"I hope so," Caroline exclaimed, picturing
all sorts of notions lining racks and cupboards.

"Course it has a general store, silly," Henry
said. "Every town does. I hope it has a tav-
ern, too. Plenty of frolics to watch in a place
like that."

"Never mind that, Henry-O," Mother said
firmly.

"I want to see stables," Thomas said. "And

horses getting their shoes put on."

"I like the blacksmith's shop, too." Joseph rumpled his little brother's hair playfully. "We can look in there together."

On they walked along the territorial road. Fewer trees dotted the landscape; hills of tall, swaying grasses brushed the rich blue depths of the early fall sky. Here and there, a cabin appeared, a barn, a little frame house. Chickens squawked and waddled across their barnyards, and occasionally a dog growled and barked suspiciously at them as they passed by.

"We must be getting closer to the cross-roads," Mother declared. "There are more and more houses lining the road. It's a sure sign."

"Look at that," Caroline said with great admiration as she noticed a lofty frame house that had just come into view. Newly built, the house stood grandly on top of a hill, overlooking the road. A wide, open porch wrapped around the spacious first floor of the house, and two opposing chimneys rose above the roof on either side, framing the tall glass windows

that sparkled out from the second floor.

"It's almost as big as Mrs. Stoddard's house," Martha observed. "I bet some fancy rich folk live inside."

"Best to be rich in good works, Martha," Mother reminded. "Let's keep walking."

"I think we're here," Joseph interrupted. Perplexed, he ran his fingers through his greased hair and pointed in front of him. "It doesn't make much sense, but the peddler told us the town would be at the crossroads."

Taken aback, Henry looked from one road to the next. "*This* can't be the crossroads of town. Nohow!" he cried. "There isn't a town here, not even one old building! Let's keep going, Joseph," he insisted. "There must be another road ahead somewhere—"

"I'm afraid your brother is right, Henry-O," Mother interrupted. "We've come to the cross-roads, so this must be the center of town. I knew Concord was small," she said, trying not to sound too disappointed. "I simply never imagined it being *this* small."

Confused, Caroline looked up at Mother.

"But there's no general store," she said. "No halfway house or stables. Where's the cobbler's shop or the doctor's house?"

"There isn't any schoolhouse, either," Eliza moaned. "I was supposed to begin lessons with Caroline and Martha next summer."

Stepping backward in disbelief, Caroline echoed her younger sister's words. "No school-house," she breathed, fanning her face with her hand. "How will we have lessons without a schoolhouse?"

"You'll have your lessons at home, just as you did for years," Mother replied. "Besides, who's to say there is no schoolhouse? I've never yet seen one built near the busy crossroads of a town. Perhaps it's off on one of these hills somewhere."

"Not one wagon, team of horses, or plain old person has passed by in all the minutes we've been standing here," Henry grumbled. "I'd hardly call that a busy crossroads."

Fidgeting nervously, Joseph looked at Mother. "What will we do with all our plans, if there's no one around to tell them to? We need a storekeeper to trade with, at least."

"We'll simply have to go to every homestead in these whereabouts until we find someone who needs our help," Mother answered determinedly. "Each of us will choose a house. Joseph, take Thomas with you. Eliza, go with Martha. Introduce yourself and ask politely if someone in the house needs help with any chores—cleaning, sewing, mending, chopping trees. Don't forget to thank whomever you speak to, whether he or she is helpful or not. And come back here to meet the rest of us as soon as you've finished your business."

"May I go to the house on the hill?" Caroline asked.

"But I want to go there!" Martha argued.

Mother quickly settled the matter. "Caroline saw the house first, Martha, and there are plenty of others to visit. Go, Caroline, and mind your manners."

"Yes, ma'am."

The grassy hill was steeper than Caroline thought. Lifting the hem of her blue dress above her ankles, she climbed through the tall, soft grass, and was nearly out of breath before she reached the top of the hill. Stopping a moment to let the breeze cool her warm face, Caroline gazed at the sky. Endlessly bright and blue all around her, it seemed close enough to touch.

Excited and nervous all at once, Caroline walked slowly toward the tall house on the hill, her heart beating loudly in her ears. She was just about to step onto the porch when she heard a quiet whimper and stopped. "Hello?" she called out softly, listening for the sound again. Instead of a whimper, she now heard the slurping of tears and scraping of leather soles on wood. Caroline turned toward the far side of the porch. The noises were coming from behind a slat-backed rocker that was rocking gently in the corner.

"Hello," Caroline said again, watching the rocker closely.

"Go 'way!" a tiny voice squeaked.

Climbing the stairs slowly, Caroline crossed the porch. "Please, can I help?" she asked gently.

The rocker slowed to a standstill. "Go 'way," the voice squeaked again.

For a moment, Caroline considered leaving, but then decided that helping this voice could be just what she'd hoped for. "Can I get someone to help you, at least?" she asked the empty rocker.

After a loud snuffle, a pixie face with tear-filled green eyes and a shock of red hair peeked out from behind the chair. "Mama needs help," the little girl said, sniffing. "Not me."

"Maybe I can help your mama," Caroline said. "Climb out from under that chair and tell me how."

"Papa says doctors help. And the Lord does, too." The child looked up at Caroline. "Who are you?" she asked.

"I'm just a girl," Caroline answered. "But I could help your mama sew or clean or cook, even."

"You have a pretty dress," the little girl said, rubbing her runny nose. "Will you play with me?"

"Course I will," Caroline said. Kneeling on the hard plank floor, she waited until the little girl crawled out from beneath the chair and stood in front of her. "First, please tell me what's happened to your mother."

"She had a baby sister for me," the little girl said solemnly. "But she's sick now. I can't see her, Papa says."

"What do you want, child?" A deep voice resonated from behind as a door closed tightly. Caroline scrambled to her feet and turned around. A tall man was standing there. His jacket covered his crisp white shirt, and his gaiters were neatly buttoned from his knees down to his boots. The man's black hair was neatly greased in smooth lines behind his ears, and even though his face looked tired and drawn, and his dark eyes were so sad, Caroline thought he was the handsomest man she'd ever seen.

"She came to play with me," the red-headed girl called out.

"Pardon me, sir," Caroline stammered, "But I came here to ask where the town is, or the general store, or someplace where someone in my family can work or trade. I heard this little girl crying on the porch and I asked her why she was so sad. She told me her mama is sick." Pausing for one quick breath, Caroline rambled on, "I could run and find a doctor for her mama, sir. That is, if you can tell me where I might find one."

"Thank you, child," the man said, "but a doctor has already been called to the house. As for the town you're looking for, I can't tell you where to find one between here and Madison."

"Maybe I could sit with the little girl until her mama is better, sir?" Caroline suggested.

"Please, Papa." The child ran to her father and pulled at his pant leg, begging, "I want to play!"

The man's face clouded with concern. "We mustn't have any visitors in our house before your mama is well again, Margaret."

The little girl buried her face in her hands. "Maybe she could play with me and my sisters at our house, sir," Caroline said, her heart aching for the crying girl. "My brothers and my mother live there, too. So does our dog, Wolf. Margaret could come anytime."

"Where is your house, child?" the man asked.

"My name's Caroline Quiner, sir, and I live no more than two miles away, as the crow flies, so my mother says."

"You've just settled in these parts?"

"We've lived here since the spring, clearing our land, sir."

"Who is looking for work or a place to trade, then?" the man asked.

"My mother, my brothers, and me and my sisters," Caroline replied. "All of us, I reckon. We lost our crop in the storm that's just passed. My mother makes dresses prettier than any you've ever looked at, and my brothers can do all the things that boys do."

"Did your mother make your dress?" the man asked.

"Yes, sir!" Caroline said proudly.

"Then you're a truthful child, since it is one of the prettiest dresses I've ever seen."

Caroline blushed and beamed at the same time. "Thank you, sir."

"Tell me, Caroline, does your mother cook as well as she sews? Or does one of your sisters, perhaps?"

"Mother's the finest, sir."

Lifting Margaret into his arms, the man smiled at Caroline. "You run along, Caroline, and tell your mother I need someone to cook for my laborers. If she agrees to work for me, I'll provide her with all the food she needs to keep those men fed, and enough for you and your family, as well."

Stunned at her good fortune, Caroline said only, "Oh, thank you, sir!"

"Kellogg's the name," the man said, laughing. "You tell one of your brothers this matter is of great shakes to me, and he must come here tomorrow to take me to your house, if your mother is interested in speaking with me. If your home is as close to the land my men are clearing as I think it is, and your mother agrees to feed them, we'll begin without delay."

"Yes, sir!" said Caroline.

"Go now, child." Mr. Kellogg shooed her away.

Waving to Margaret, Caroline hurried down the hill toward the crossroads. Mother's wise words rang in her ears over and over again: "Be not forgetful to entertain strangers, for thereby some have entertained angels unawares." Mother was always right!

Hired Hands

The next morning, Mother used the last of her white flour to make hotcakes. "Nothing leaves a home smelling sweeter than hotcakes," she said as Caroline and her sisters took turns dipping their hands into the washbasin and splashing their sleepy faces with cool water. "I only wish I had a few slices of salt pork to cook as well." Humming to herself, Mother bustled about, whipping the creamy batter, scooping spoonfuls of lard into the skillet and swirling around the sizzling fat as it melted.

Caroline pulled a stack of dishes off the dish dresser and slowly crossed to the table. "Mr. Kellogg comes today!" she said excitedly.

"Henry-O will fetch him soon as he finishes his meal," Mother replied. "I hope your Mr. Kellogg is still able to visit this morning. The peddler told us he was a mighty important man in these parts. It could be his schedule won't permit him to look in on us as planned."

"He told me to send Henry or Joseph to his house quick as possible," Caroline said as she set the plates neatly around the table. "He said he was in a hurry to find someone to feed his laborers."

"Well, I've never cooked meals for a team of hired hands before," Mother admitted, "though I imagine it's not all that different from feeding a clan of children. I'm eager to hear his proposal."

Martha set forks and tin cups beside the plates, then looked over at Mother. "Are you going to feed him some of your hotcakes?" she asked. "I would, if I were you. He can't help but think they're the tastiest fixens ever, and have you cook for all his folks after he takes one bite."

Mother laughed and began pouring shimmering round circles of batter into the bubbling fat. "I'm hoping the smell of the hotcakes in the cabin will be enough to convince him of that, since we can't wait for him to eat. Sit down now, children, we must finish our breakfast and begin tidying the house before our visitor comes."

As soon as Henry wolfed down the last of his hotcakes and wiped the drips of sugar syrup off his chin, he stood up to leave.

"Remember your manners, please," Mother warned.

"I'll be sweeter than a honeycomb," Henry promised. "And I'll use every bit of manners I ever learned if your cooking will save me from chopping trees all day or hauling in a harvest for some farmer I don't know from a grizzly."

Tapping her chin, Mother raised one eyebrow as she looked up at her son. "Maybe

Joseph should go instead," she considered.

"I'll talk like a book, I promise!" Henry insisted. "By the time we come back, old Kellogg will set much store by me. You'll see."

"Be on your way then," Mother said. She stood up and pushed Henry's honey-colored curls out of his eyes. "And please don't refer to him as 'old' when you meet him."

Their stomachs warm and full, Joseph and Thomas went to do the outside chores while Caroline, Martha, and Eliza cleared the table, scrubbed and dried the dishes, then set out to sweep the plank floors, tidy the rooms, and make the beds.

"I hope he'll come," Martha whispered to Caroline as they pulled the pillows off the beds, pinched their corners, and fluffed them into soft square puffs. "Mother's so happy all of a sudden."

"He said he would, and I believe him."

Just as the girls finished their chores, Henry flung the door open, announcing their arrival. "We're here!" he cried.

Smoothing her apron over her skirt, Mother

hurried across the room. "Welcome, Mr. Kellogg," she said warmly. "Please come in. Henry, go call your brothers."

"Yes, ma'am," Henry said. "It was mighty fine walking and speaking with you, sir," he added. Then he dashed out the door.

Standing alone in front of the doorway, Mr. Kellogg looked even taller than Caroline remembered, almost too big for the room. Beneath his smoke-colored roundabout, he wore a pale-gray shirt. His long black trousers hung straight to the toes of his black ankle boots. Removing his black hat, he stepped toward Mother. "A fine boy, ma'am," he said, smoothing his hair where his hat had left a ring of flattened black locks. "And it is I who should welcome you. Your daughter told me you've recently settled in these parts."

"He's dashing!" Martha whispered into Caroline's ear.

"We arrived with the spring," Mother answered, glancing severely at Caroline and Martha to stifle their giggles.

"Would that our weather had treated you

better in your first planting season," Mr. Kellogg said. "I haven't seen such powerful hot and dry days since I settled in these parts. Most every evening since we dug and planted our acres, I've had men dragging water from the river to keep corn and the like growing. If I'd had to tend the crops alone, I'd have lost it all, too."

Surprised, Mother asked, "The storm didn't cause you any loss then?"

"On the contrary, ma'am. It destroyed a good amount of our yield, but I still had many crops that fared just fine. Even folks like you who lost most of their harvest didn't have it as bad as some. Story has it a farmer and his missus in Watertown lost their entire home-stead to a tornado that whupped through dur-ing the storm. It's our good fortune the twister steered clear of Concord."

"And your wife, sir?" Mother asked gently. "Caroline tells me she's taken ill."

"Soon after the birth of our second child," Mr. Kellogg said. "Laura would have welcomed you to Concord herself, had she been able."

"If I can help, or the children, perhaps—" Mother began.

"It's in the good Lord's hands, as they say," their guest replied. "Thank you for your kind offer." Glancing about the room, Mr. Kellogg spotted Caroline, and his mood lightened immediately. "Good morning to you, Caroline! These must be the sisters you told me about."

"Yes, sir," Caroline said, pleased that such an important man had remembered her name. "This is Martha. She's the oldest girl. And here's Eliza. She's littler than I am, of course."

Mr. Kellogg listened carefully. "A pleasure, young ladies," he said, nodding to them. "Which one of you made this home smell so delightful?"

The three girls sang out, "Mother!"

Mr. Kellogg grinned and followed Mother to the table, where they sat down across from each other. "Which brings me to the very reason I've come," he said. "Caroline tells me you're looking for work, Mrs. Quiner."

"Yes, I am."

"As I told your daughter, ma'am, I need to

find someone to cook for my five laborers. You'll have to make three hearty meals every day but Sabbaday until my wife's able to feed the men again herself. Far as I can tell, you're no more than a mile from the land we're clearing. The men could walk here easy. I'll be certain to send enough food to keep the workers and your family fed, and pay you a fair wage as well. You'd be doing me an almighty favor, ma'am, should you choose to help."

"As would you, sir, by having me help," Mother said gratefully. "When shall we begin?"

"If that's a yes, Mrs. Quiner, tomorrow I'll have the men begin toting you a right smart of bushels, fresh from the harvest. They'll begin taking meals here Monday next."

"That gives us three days. We'll be prepared," Mother said.

The door slammed shut behind Mr. Kellogg, and he shifted on his chair to find Henry, Joseph, and Thomas watching him. "*Three* boys!" he exclaimed. "I'll have to send more food than I planned."

"We could help with any chores you might

be needing help with, sir," Joseph said readily. "Chopping up timber, for instance."

"Thank you, son. But I imagine your mother will use all the logs you can split, just to keep the cookstove and the fire burning. You could possibly help me by hunting small game for her, however."

"Last year we caught more passenger pigeons than you've seen in all your born days, Mr. Kellogg," Henry broke in. "We sold them at a good lay for more than ten whole dollars! Are you the one who collects the birds in this town?"

"I'm afraid we don't sell passenger pigeons to anybody here," Mr. Kellogg said. "We're too far from a port that ships them. We do, however, eat plenty of birds in stews and pies. I'll pay you the same amount, Henry, to keep your mother supplied with barrels full of those pigeons that she can feed to my men."

"Yes, sir!"

"I stack little logs for the fire sometimes," Thomas chimed in.

"A good log stacker is near impossible to

find, lad," Mr. Kellogg answered seriously. "Take pride in hard work well done." Standing up, he placed his hat on his head. "I'll take my leave then, Mrs. Quiner, trusting that you'll send one of the boys for me if a problem arises."

"Without question." Mother walked her guest to the door and closed it behind him after a final good-bye. Whirling around, she jigged across the room, her skirt swinging merrily. "We've found work, children!" she exclaimed joyfully. "Hard work, yes, but work nonetheless. Beginning tomorrow, we will have enough food on our table to feed a forest full of wildcats. Thank you, Caroline, for finding our Mr. Kellogg!"

Giddy with delight, Caroline took hold of Mother's hands and danced about the room with her, whirling, whirling, whirling, until she fell into Mother's arms for a warm, lasting hug.

Mr. Kellogg was as good as his word. The sun had just peeked above the forest on the edge of the clearing when Caroline heard the sound of men's voices thundering through the trees.

"Go! Get back in your house now," she told the hens as she shooed them into their wooden box. "Mr. Kellogg's men are coming to bring us food, and I don't want them mistaking you for chickens they're planning to eat!"

Standing guard in front of the henhouse door, Caroline watched as four men stomped across the clearing, their arms heavy with bushels, baskets, pails, and sacks. A fifth man, leading a cow with one hand and balancing a crate of squawking chickens on his shoulder with the other, trailed the rest.

"You there, little girl," a gruff voice shouted. "Where should we put these?"

"Think quick, girlie," a second voice burst out. "I snore these sacks are gol-derned heavy."

Stunned by the men's rudeness, Caroline opened her mouth to speak, but nothing came out. She was about to run for Henry and Joseph when the man leading the cow spoke up.

"Mind your tongues in front of the young

lady," he ordered. "And leave the food over by the house. The missus will say what to do with it. You come with me, Addie," he said, pulling the cow toward Caroline.

Caroline backed up against the chickens' box as the man moved closer, towering over her. Wide-set blue eyes stood out above the man's square, clean-shaven cheeks. His brown hair was neatly combed off his high forehead and hung straight to his chin. The bushy strip of hair framing his jaw reminded Caroline of a furry brown caterpillar. The man spoke quietly and never smiled. "That's a box full of hens behind you there. Am I right, little girl?"

The word "no" on the tip of her tongue, Caroline paused just long enough for muffled squawks and clucks to filter through wooden doors. "Yes, sir," she admitted guiltily.

"Don't want you to use your birds to feed us," the man said. "So I've brought more. If you are their caretaker, keep their crate close to yours. Makes feedin' and cleanin' easier. Just don't get them all mixed up with each other. And be certain to say when you need more."

"Thank you, sir," Caroline said, watching the man's big callused hands as he gently laid the crate full of gibbering hens beside her on the dark soil and peered inside.

"They made the short trip with no harm done," he said. "Can you point me to your barn now, miss? I'd like to get Addie here all set before I take my leave."

"We don't have a barn," Caroline said.

"A shanty or a lean-to then," the man answered. "Someplace where she'll be sheltered from the cold winds and snow."

Caroline shook her head.

"Nothing here on your land?" he asked, searching the stump-spotted clearing.

"No, sir."

"We'll have to build a pole barn for Addie then, before the weather turns cold. Otherways, Kellogg will tell me to return her to his homestead, and we'll have no butter or milk for our meals. Let's leave her out back till I find me the time to build her some shelter."

"We put all the fixens where you told us, Holbrook," a gruff voice interrupted from behind them. Caroline looked at the short man who was speaking. His shaggy head of hair and the speckled beard sprouting from his puffy cheeks and chin hid most of his face, but she could clearly see his black eyes darting about as he spoke. Caroline quickly decided she didn't like those eyes.

"Some boys out by the woodpile says they'll move 'em wherever their mother says," the scruffy man continued. "The rest of us is leaving now. You coming, Holbrook?"

"I'll see to Addie, and then I'll be along."

"Hirch says we meet here, dinnertime tomorrow."

"Hirch doesn't know beans from buckshot," Mr. Holbrook scoffed. "Kellogg wants us back here first light, day after tomorrow. That's *two* sunrises from now. Tell the others."

The short man made a loud gurgling sound in the back of his throat, spit at the dirt, then wiped his chin with the back of his hand. He whistled the other three men to his side, and they walked into the forest, chattering raucously.

"Pay them no mind, little girl," Mr. Holbrook said. "A man's not born with manners, after all. Hirch and his mate, Burgg, never bothered to learn any."

"Caroline?" Mother walked up swiftly beside her and laid a firm hand on her shoulder. "Come along now, if you've finished tending the hens. It's dinnertime, almost."

"Yes, ma'am. I'm finished."

"Along with the rest of the food and these hens, Mrs. Quiner, Mr. Kellogg sent this cow," Mr. Holbrook told Mother. "I was just telling your little girl that I'll have to build you a pole barn before the cold weather comes."

"She's not come for butchering, then?"

"No, ma'am. Addie's due to bring another calf into the world come spring. Till then, she'll be supplying our milk and butter. She'll need shelter."

"My boys can build a shelter," Mother replied. "No sense in adding more work to all you have to do for Mr. Kellogg."

"Happy to help, ma'am. Addie's a favorite of mine, and I can't help but like fresh butter with my meals."

"We're grateful for your help, then," Mother relented. "Thank you, Mr. . . ."

"Holbrook, ma'am. You're most welcome. Good day to you and the young lady," he said, handing Mother the twine he had strung around Addie's wrinkly brown neck.

Caroline and Mother watched Mr. Holbrook cross the clearing and disappear into the woods. "He's nice," Caroline said as they steered the cow out back of the cabin. "The others are awful."

"Nonsense! We have a cow, a crate of hens, sacks of flour and sugar, and bushels full of corn and vegetables!" Mother exclaimed. "How blessed we are, Caroline! Now we must get to work preparing bread and pies and the like, and hope the Lord will forgive us for working on His day of rest. Monday morning will come sooner than we think."

The warm sun slipped behind a sloping mound of burly white clouds. The brisk fall breeze hit Caroline full in the face. Rubbing her hand over Addie's velvety dark hide, she shivered. Mr. Holbrook had been nice enough, but two of the other men had frightened her. Caroline didn't want them in her house or eating at her table. But she kept her thoughts to herself and listened to Mother's cheerful chatter, hoping that Monday morning would be a longer time coming than Mother thought.

Servings

"The scalded milk must be blood-warm by now, Caroline," Mother said. "Mix it with the yeast and set it aside to soak. Then make a well in the center of the flour-and-salt mixture. Crumble a small chunk of sugar into the flour well; it will help the yeast swell the bread dough faster and make the loaves a prettier, brown. Add the butter and the yeast mixture to the flour, and stir it until you've formed a ball of dough. Cover it; then set it aside to rise." Pausing for a moment, Mother studied Caroline's face.

"Did I say too much too fast, Caroline?" she asked.

"No, ma'am," Caroline answered, Mother's words jumping about in her head like grasshoppers.

Satisfied, Mother returned to the far side of the table and began patching her pie dough with extra pieces of the rich puff paste she had just mixed together. "Good."

Concentrating as hard as she could, Caroline tried to remember all of Mother's instructions. She had never made bread dough by herself before, but Mother had far too much work to do in one day, and she needed all the girls to help her. While Martha churned the cream into butter, Eliza sorted dried huckleberries for Mother to bake in her pies. Caroline stood on the opposite side of the table from Mother, staring at the flour and salt in her bowl as she repeated Mother's steps to herself.

"First, the yeast," she said. "Mix it with the milk." Dabbing her fingertip into the small iron pot in front of her, Caroline determined the scalded milk was indeed blood-warm, and crumbled two small yeast cakes into it. "Let it soak now, and make the well," she murmured. Moving the yeast mixture aside, she turned to the bowl of flour and salt, sifted them together with her fingers, and pressed the grainy powder down in the center with her knuckles, creating a deep, wide pocket.

Think, think, think, Caroline thought. Oh, yes, sugar! She reached for the iron tongs that Mother had left beside the tall white cone in the middle of the table, stood on her tiptoes, and broke off a chunk of sugar from the sparkly tip. Crumbling it between her fingertips, she scattered the white crystals over the flour, then looked from mixing bowl to iron pot. The yeast and milk have to go into the well now, she remembered. Then I can mix it all up. Slowly, Caroline poured the creamy liquid into the powder, and began stirring it round and round with her long-handled spoon. Mounds of flour clinging to the sides of the bowl slid down to the liquid center. Caroline kept stirring until all the flour and liquid had thickened into a stiff, sticky clump of dough.

Releasing the spoon, she rubbed her sore upper arm and realized she couldn't remember what to do next.

"I made a dough ball," Caroline told Mother. "What should I do now?"

"Sprinkle a handful of flour over the dough so it won't stick to the bowl anymore," Mother instructed as she pressed the edge of her flaky pie paste together and crimped it with her fingers. "Then cover it with one of my clean rags and set it on the dish dresser to rise. You can prepare another bread dough while you wait for the first to double in size, Caroline. Then it will be ready to knead and bake."

Surprised, Caroline glanced across the room at Martha. Mother had never mentioned making more than one ball of bread dough.

"Maybe I could make the next bread dough, and Caroline could churn butter for a while," Martha quickly suggested. Standing near the fiery hearth, the churn dash in her hand, she pushed clinging wet strands of hair off her forehead and flushed cheeks. "I think the butter's almost ready, anyhow," she said. "Some of it's sticking to the bottom of the stick. It won't take much longer now."

"If it's all right with your sister, Martha, it's fine with me," Mother said. "Just decide quickly."

Caroline couldn't make up her mind. Stirring the flour and yeast-milk mixture made her arm ache, but she loved the rich, yeasty smell of the dough. If she churned butter, she'd get to see the creamy yellow lumps separate from the frothy buttermilk, but she'd have to stand near the blazing hearth to do it. Caroline almost decided to continue her mixing and stirring, but Martha looked so hot and tired, she couldn't bring herself to do it. "We can switch," she said. Clapping a dusting of flour off her hands, she covered her dough ball, left it on the dish dresser, and headed for the hearth.

"Do you think we'll have this much work to do every day?" Martha whispered to Caroline.

"I hope not," Caroline whispered back. Seating herself on a rickety old stool in front of the butter churn, she tipped the cover off and peered inside to see if any lumps of butter were forming yet. A few small yellow grains glistened on the bottom of the dash, but the creamy buttermilk was free of any floating clumps. "It'll take longer than you think it will, Martha," she grumbled to herself.

Pressing her flattened palms against the wooden churn-dash, Caroline began rolling it swiftly between her fingers. She rolled and rolled until her palms became hot and tingly, then she stood up and pumped the dash up and down, beating the cream as flames leaped and crackled in the hearth at her side. Drips of sweat soon slipped down her face and neck, but Caroline paid them no mind. Almost out of breath, she peeked beneath the lid again, and sighed with relief when she spotted small bits of butter floating in the buttermilk.

"I need the trough," Caroline called out. "The butter's ready."

"I'll help," Martha offered. "The bread dough is finished, too."

"I picked through all the berries," Eliza spoke up. "Can I help with the butter, too?"

"Take this empty can and begin cutting

dumplings out of this dough," Mother told her youngest daughter. "Martha can help Caroline just fine."

Martha carried a narrow, rectangular trough to the table. Together she and Caroline lifted the small churn and tilted it over the trough, straining the buttermilk from the butter and pouring it back into the churn.

"I can finish now," Caroline said. Three lumps of butter rested in the trough, and she poured jug after jug of water over the butter, washing it again and again until the butter melded into one large clump and the water she poured over it remained clear. Using the back of a wooden spoon, Caroline pressed the butter clump as hard as she could, squeezing all the remaining buttermilk out of it. Then she poured the last drops of the creamy liquid back into the churn and washed the butter one last time.

"The water in the trough is clear, so I'm ready to salt the butter," she told Mother. "How much should I put in?"

"Are you certain you squeezed all the

buttermilk out of the butter?" Mother asked. "It will leave a bad taste otherwise."

Without answering, Caroline stood on her tiptoes over the trough and pushed the back of the wooden spoon on the butter until her face turned red with the effort. "There's no more buttermilk in there. There's no liquid at all, hardly."

"Good. Then add three pinches of salt," Mother said. Leaning over the row of pies on the table in front of her, Mother looked on as Caroline reached into the salt box on the mantelpiece, gathered a small amount of salt into her palm, then sprinkled three pinches of the sandy white grains over the butter. "That's enough," Mother cautioned. "Now spoon it into one of the firkins."

Caroline did as she was told, then proudly handed a small tub of creamy yellow butter to Mother.

"It's perfect," Mother praised. "Fresh creamy butter, and still a pretty yellow, too. Once the weather grows cold and the cream is white again, we'll have to color it with carrot juice to get this yellow color, Caroline. I only wish I could find my wooden butter molds to press it in."

"Did you lose them?" Caroline asked.

"It's been so long since we've had a cow to milk, I can't remember where I put them for safekeeping. I fear they never made the move with us from Brookfield." Mother sighed. They were all silent for a moment, thinking about their old home.

"I bet Mr. Ben has them," Martha said. "He always brought us cream from his cows to churn into butter. Maybe you gave him the molds to say thank you for all that cream."

"No." Mother dismissed the notion. "I would certainly have remembered that."

"All the times I ever helped churn Mr. Ben's cream, we never made pretty prints out of it," Caroline said.

Shaking her head, Mother said, "Perhaps they'll surprise us and reappear someday, but we haven't time to concern ourselves now. We have cucumbers to pickle and eggs to stuff, turnips to mash and potatoes to peel.

The day's wasting, girls."

For the rest of the day and long into the evening, while their brothers split logs for the cookstove and hearth fire, Caroline and her sisters kneaded bread dough, washed and peeled turnips and potatoes, boiled eggs, and mashed their yolks for stuffing. They straightened and swept the cabin from top to bottom, and scrutinized every tin cup and plate Mother owned to be certain it was clean.

Except for the golden flames vaulting around the sputtering logs in the hearth, the cabin was dark and full of shifting shadows when the girls finally pulled their nightgowns over their heads, tied their nightcaps, and tumbled into bed exhausted.

"I hurt all over," Martha complained as she dropped her head into her pillow.

"Me, too," Eliza said between yawns.

"And Mr. Kellogg's men aren't even here yet," Caroline said, stretching out her cramped muscles. "Tomorrow we'll have to serve those folks and clean all their dirty dishes, too."

"For three whole meals," Martha added.

"Just remember not to look at any of them while they are eating," Mother said from the doorway, where she was leaning her head against the door and listening. "It's a terribly rude thing to do."

"I'm sorry for complaining, ma'am," Caroline said. She didn't know that Mother had been listening, and would have kept all her complaints to herself if she had.

"I'm so bone-tired, I can think of a few complaints myself," Mother said.

Caroline smiled in the darkness. The thought of Mother wanting to complain made her feel much better.

"Let us not be weary in well-doing, however," Mother gently reminded her. "Mr. Kellogg is certainly helping us, but we are doing a good turn for him and his family, as well."

"Yes, ma'am," Caroline replied sleepily. She liked Mr. Kellogg and Margaret, and wanted to help them. She only wished that helping them wasn't such hard work.

* * *

Early the next morning, the little cabin buzzed with activity. Joseph stoked the fire and piled oak logs into the hearth while Henry filled the cookstove with green hardwood logs that would burn slowly through the morning. Mother whipped flour, salt, eggs, saleratus, and buttermilk into a frothy batter for buckwheat hotcakes. Martha stood watch over a skillet of sizzling fried salt pork and drippings. Caroline helped Eliza neatly set the table and stirred the porridge simmering on the cookstove. Thomas carefully carried the firkin of butter, and a piggin each of preserves and sugar syrup, to the center of the table.

The dawn was just beginning to nudge away the darkness when Mr. Kellogg's men arrived. Barking their good mornings, the men took seats at the table. Mr. Holbrook arrived last. "A good morning to you, Mrs. Quiner," he said, "and to the children. Thank you for assisting us so."

"You're welcome, Mr. Holbrook," Mother said, looking startled. "Please sit down before your food is too cold to eat."

"Dig in!" A deep voice shouted the moment Mr. Holbrook was seated.

Standing on the far side of the room, opposite the door, Caroline bowed her head and tried not to look at the men around the table. "They didn't even say grace," she whispered to Martha.

"Mind your manners, Blue," Mr. Holbrook remarked. "We're in the presence of a lady and her children. Say your grace."

"This beats the Dutch!" a gruff voice scoffed. Caroline immediately recognized it as Mr. Hirch's. "Blue would as soon say grace as I might catch a weasel asleep!"

"Then he'll shut pan and put his fork on his plate till the rest of us say ours," Holbrook said firmly.

"Let Holbrook say his grace," Mr. Burgg interrupted, "so *he'll* shut pan and I can eat."

The room was suddenly silent as Mr. Holbrook bowed his head and prayed, "Be present at this table, Lord. Amen."

Mother continued to fry hotcakes as the men began chomping, slurping, clanging forks,

and smacking their lips. Caroline carried plateful after plateful of steaming hotcakes to the
table, only to have them disappear immediately. Once, she set a full platter in front of
the shaggy Mr. Burgg and caught her breath
as he dug his knife into the top of the pile,
scooped up four cakes, and dropped them on
his plate. After slathering a pat of butter over
them, he cut them into long strips, elbows
high in the air, then shoveled them into his
mouth with his knife. Caroline couldn't help
staring as some strips of the cakes slipped off
the knife and fell to the floor below. Seated
on the edge of his chair at quite a distance
from the table, Mr. Burgg never noticed half
his hotcakes disappearing between his legs.
But he did notice Caroline.

"Get us more fixens, little girl," he said,
grabbing his fork and using it to pick at his
teeth.

"Yes, sir," Caroline said, and she hurried
back to the stove.

"Did you see what that man with the long
whiskers did after I poured him his coffee?"

Martha whispered as Mother filled Caroline's empty plate with buckwheat hotcakes. "He gulped it so fast, he scalded his mouth. Then he coughed and sprayed his coffee all over your piggin of preserves!"

"I expect you girls to keep the men fed," Mother said sharply, "not to watch their manners."

"Flapjacks, girlie!" a voice rang out. "Shouldn't take a coon's age to get fixens on the table!"

Caroline swallowed her growing anger and quickly carried the plate of hotcakes to the table.

"Is thar more coffee brewing in this hum, or ain't thar?" an angry voice shouted, and a tin cup came clattering down on the table.

"Yes, sir." Caroline turned to the pallid-faced man who had just banged his empty cup on the table and politely answered him over the din. "My sister will fetch it for you in a minute, if you please."

"Such good eats, they're a-calling me to finish the last o' the sweet syrup right off my plate," a lanky man seated at the corner of the table told Caroline. Lifting his plate to his mouth, he leisurely licked the last drops of syrup off it and smacked his lips. "I couldna eat one more morsel," he sighed, and he handed Caroline his plate.

Horrified, Caroline dropped the sticky, wet plate. Motionless with dismay, she listened as the plate rattled and clanged on the wooden boards before lying silent.

"What kind of help's Kellogg got us this time?" Mr. Hirch complained. "Next meal, we'll have to cook and clear the table for ourselves, and *then* clear his land!"

Caroline jumped as a fist slammed the table with a thunderous crash. "Enough!" Mr. Holbrook said between clenched teeth. "These are the best doings we've had to eat since the day we started working for Kellogg. Any man who disagrees ought to say so now."

The fat in the skillet popped. The shifting logs in the hearth hissed. But no one spoke.

Mr. Holbrook stood up and wiped his lips and chin with his napkin. Turning to Mother, who was standing by the cookstove, he folded his napkin and placed it on his empty plate. "Thank you kindly for the meal, ma'am," he said. "I'll be returning for dinner this noon, and bringing any man here who's got manners and shows some respect along with me. The rest will fix their meals for their ungrateful selves."

"Thank you, Mr. Holbrook," Mother said, her face pale and her jaw set. "I trust that you'll keep your word."

"Yes, ma'am." Mr. Holbrook nodded, and he left the cabin. The rest of the men rose from their seats silently and headed for the door, murmuring their thanks to Mother.

"I have half a mind to send Henry for Mr. Kellogg this minute and tell him I'll have no part in cooking for such folk!" Mother snapped, and she tossed her wooden spoon into the empty batter bowl. "The very thought of having such men in my home!"

"Mr. Holbrook will help us," Caroline said. "He won't let those men talk to us like that anymore."

"I must remember, pride goeth before a fall," Mother resolved. Brushing the damp hair off her forehead and rubbing her eyes, she added, "We'll give it two weeks."

Scrubbing the hotcake strips, salt pork drippings, crusted preserves, and hard cold mush that were stuck to the floor planks beneath the table, Caroline thought long and hard. She couldn't imagine what pride had to do with Mr. Kellog's hired hands and their dreadful manners. All she knew was that it was going to be a long two weeks.

Pole Barn

The winds became brisk, the air shivery. The forest's brown leaves whirled to the ground without ever having a chance to show their splendid fall colors. They skipped about the woods, leaving the bare branches above them waiting for the first winter snow.

Two long months had passed, and Mother was still feeding Mr. Kellogg's hired hands. Caroline spent most of her days inside, peeling vegetables, kneading dough, churning fresh butter, serving meals, and cleaning up after the workers. Each week she counted the moments until Sunday, when Mother insisted that the children spend the morning learning Bible verses and the afternoon resting or playing quietly outside. "The Lord never worked on Sunday," Mother would say. "It is proper and right that we follow His example." It wasn't until late Sunday evenings, when the tiny bedroom was dark and Caroline was tucked in beside her sisters, that Mother herself would bustle about the cookstove once again.

One Sunday morning, Mother sat at the head of the table, listening closely as the children recited their verses.

"Mine's a long one today," Caroline said when it was her turn. Then she began speaking each word carefully. "'Inasmuch as ye have done it unto one of the least of these my . . .'" She paused, uncertain how to say the word that followed.

"'Brethren,'" Mother pronounced. "It means brothers."

"'. . . brethren, ye have done it unto me,'" Caroline continued, and then she repeated the entire verse. "That's what mine says. Your turn, Martha."

"I picked a short one," Martha said. Then she slowly recited, "'Thou shalt love thy neighbor as thyself.'"

"The verse may be short, Martha," Mother declared, "but it's one of the most important to remember."

"We've all said ours twice now," Henry said, trying to curb his impatience. "That means they're stuck in our heads good. Can we be finished, Mother?"

"After you tell me the meaning of Caroline's verse, Henry-O," Mother challenged.

Surprised, Henry furrowed his brow, thinking. "It means if you do something to my littlest brother, then you're doing it to me, too," he said simply. "So if we can be finished now, I promise I won't let anything happen to Thomas that isn't a good thing to have happen to me. And I'll even love all my neighbors for Martha, too. How's that?"

"*That* is only partially correct," Mother answered, her lips curving into a smile. "Think about it some more while you're outside this morning. You may give me a more suitable answer at dinner."

"Yes, ma'am," Henry cried exuberantly, bounding out of his chair. "Let's play drop the handkerchief!" Mother looked at him sternly, her face telling him he was speaking too loudly.

"I want to play," Eliza whispered.

"Not me," Joseph replied. "I'm going to sweep up the hay for Addie, or she'll have no place to sleep."

"It's the Lord's day, children," Mother reminded them. "I expect you to play quietly. And wear your shawls and jackets. The wind is biting."

"I'll get the handkerchief," Martha said.

The five players quickly pulled on their coats and shawls, and were soon standing in a circle outside the little cabin, bouncing up and down to keep warm. "You be It first, Martha, since you have the handkerchief," Henry said.

The wind tossing the ends of her scarf all

about, Martha skipped past each player, finally dropped the handkerchief behind Thomas, and then doubled her speed. Caroline, Henry, and Eliza pretended not to see the cloth, and Martha dashed around the circle, giggling and whooping, until she arrived back at Thomas and grabbed the gray linen handkerchief off the cold earth.

"Get in the mush pot, Thomas!" Martha cried, pushing her little brother into the middle of the circle as she jumped between Caroline and Eliza into Thomas's empty spot.

Stamping his foot, Thomas yelled, "I don't want to be in a mush pot! Why do I have to go in a mush pot?"

"Because you didn't know I dropped the handkerchief behind you, and you didn't pick it up," Martha explained. "You have to pay attention, or you'll be in the mush pot all afternoon! Now be quiet, Thomas. I get to be It again."

Thomas sulked as Martha circled the players. Out of the corner of her eye, Caroline saw her sister lean over when she passed. A flash of gray fell to the ground behind her, and she was just about to whirl around to snatch the handkerchief when Thomas yelled again, "I don't want to stay in the mush pot!"

Standing her ground, Caroline waited until Martha ran up and slapped her on the shoulder. "I thought *you* knew how to play this game, at least," Martha teased. "Your turn in the mush pot, Caroline!"

Caroline was just about to tell Martha that she knew the handkerchief was there all along when Thomas shouted happily, "Come in here, Caroline, so I can play."

Caroline looked from Martha's gloating face to Thomas's shining one. "Take my place, Thomas," Caroline said, "and make sure you watch where the handkerchief drops."

"Martha's going to be It forever," Henry grumbled. "Move on before I'm too frozen to play anymore!"

Once in the middle of the circle, Caroline stood with her back to the cabin, facing Henry and the woods. The winter sun cast shimmering rays through the leafless black trees, dimly lighting the forest. As Martha raced around the circle yet again, humming loudly, Caroline spied a man walking toward them through the trees.

"Someone's coming," Caroline said, squinting to see better.

Eliza seized the handkerchief Martha had dropped behind her and scampered around the circle after Martha. "You didn't pick me because you knew I'd catch you!" Henry shouted at Martha.

The figure in the woods moved closer, and Caroline finally recognized the man's neatly combed brown hair and the bushy strip of a beard that lined his jaw. "Look, it's Mr. Holbrook," she said, pointing. "He's coming through the woods."

"What for?" Henry asked as Martha and Eliza came to a quick halt and looked. "We're not supposed to feed anybody but ourselves on Sunday!"

"He's the nicest one of all those workers, Henry," Caroline said.

"If it wasn't for Mr. Holbrook, the rest of

those men would still be treating us like a boodle of servants," Martha agreed. "Wait and see what he's come for, Henry, before you get yourself in such a bother."

Carrying a broadaxe in one hand, Mr. Holbrook walked briskly toward the cabin, an adze and an auger tilting out of the sack he had tied around his waist. "Good day, children," he said when he came upon the circle. "I've come to build a pole barn for Addie before the cold gets any worse. If you will, son, show me where to find some suitable timber."

"Name's Henry, mister," Henry said sharply. "My brother and I can build our own shelter for the cow. But not today, nohow."

Mr. Holbrook studied Henry closely to determine whether or not he was telling the truth. "Are you speaking gum to me, boy?" he finally asked.

"I don't tell lies to nobody, mister," Henry answered defensively. "Mother says no work on Sunday. It's not right nor proper. The Lord Himself says so."

"I see." Mr. Holbrook began rubbing his chin hair with the back of his hand. "The Lord Himself also expects us to take care of the livestock he gives us for food and drink. And unless I build Addie a pole barn in the darkness 'fore breakfast one morn, or in the darkness one evening after clearing Kellogg's land, it won't get built any day but Sabbaday. I'll keep hope that the Lord and your mother will forgive me for working such, but I'm building that shelter today. Now where's the timber, Henry?"

"It's out back of the house, behind the wood-pile," Henry said. "Mr. Ben told us to save it till spring, when he comes back and we build a reg'lar-size barn."

"We'll only need a bit of hardwood for a pole barn," Mr. Holbrook promised. "And I'll chop you the same amount myself so it will weather before spring. Your Mr. Ben won't know the difference."

"I'll take you to the woodpile, then," Henry agreed. "I'll even help, if Mother says it's all right."

"If you've got a straw stack or a pile of hay somewheres, maybe you can bring us enough of one or the other to bed the cow," Mr. Holbrook said, looking at Caroline and Martha. "I'd prefer to use straw, but either will be a mighty help."

"Joseph keeps a small pile of hay where Addie sleeps now, but there's not near enough to fill even a pole barn. And we have no straw," Martha answered.

"Cornstalks, then?" Mr. Holbrook asked. "Did you save any of the stalks after you harvested your corn?"

"They're out back by the woodpile too," Henry said. "Mother wants to push them between the logs in the walls, and block the hides covering the windows with them so the cold can't get inside."

"Fine," Mr. Holbrook said. "We'll heap just a few of those stalks over the roof." Turning his attention to Caroline and her sisters, Mr. Holbrook said, "Perhaps you can walk along the edge of the forest and bring back any tall grasses you find. We can use them to fill the feed box and spread over the cold ground of the pole barn."

Without even asking Mother's permission, Caroline, Martha, and Eliza ran off through the clearing.

"There's grass everywhere!" Eliza cried, pointing to the yellow-brown stalks swaying between the tree stumps in the clearing.

"It's hard to . . . pull . . . OUT!" Caroline yelped, and she tumbled backward as the handful of grass she was tugging finally tore free from the cold black earth.

"Let's make one big pile here, then go find more," Martha suggested. "Mr. Holbrook says we should look close to the forest."

Caroline, Martha, and Eliza walked along the edge of the woods, yanking all the tall grasses they could find. They kicked through piles of crackling brown leaves, searching for more grass beneath them. When they had collected almost more than their arms could hold, the girls ran back to the cabin, the dry, fringed grass in their arms tickling their cold faces and chins.

As soon as the girls had tossed all their grass into a big pile out back of the cabin, Thomas began jumping into it. Mr. Holbrook, Henry, and Joseph had split the timber before the girls returned and were now stacking poles side by side into a large rectangle, and hammering them together with nails that Mr. Holbrook pulled from his pocket.

"It's our good fortune that Kellogg supplied us with these nails," Mr. Holbrook remarked as he pounded them into the wood, "or we'd be tying these poles together and hoping they'd stand through the winter."

"He's rich, isn't he?" Henry asked.

"Kellogg can plank down more money for notions than anybody I ever seen, if that's what you're asking," Mr. Holbrook answered. "Whether that makes him a rich man isn't for me to say."

"Mother says it's best to be rich in good works," Martha said knowingly.

"Your mother's wise," Mr. Holbrook replied.

"Why is there a big hole in front?" Eliza asked, pointing to the large opening in the center of the wall facing the back of the cabin.

"That's how we'll get in and out to feed Addie," Joseph answered.

"But the snow and ice will get in that way, too," Caroline reasoned. "Same as if there wasn't any shelter at all."

Mr. Holbrook paused from his hammering and turned to the girls. "A pole barn is supposed to shield the cow from the harshest snows and winds and cold, but it's not near as good a shelter as a real barn," he explained. "Addie will be just fine here until spring. Her hide will keep her plenty warm, no matter what blows in that doorway."

The rectangle of poles was now standing firm. Mr. Holbrook and Joseph began hoisting more timber over the top of the poles, laying the logs next to each other until they covered the walls to make a roof. Once the little dwelling was complete, Mr. Holbrook tossed an armful of stalks over the top and tied them down with heavy twine.

"Any stalks left over after your mother covers the openings in the house, wrap and tie them to each of these standing poles," Mr. Holbrook advised the boys. "It'll keep the inside warmer for Addie."

"I'll do that, sir," Joseph promised.

"Now," Mr. Holbrook continued, "let's get the feed box inside and line the ground with the grass. If I have time 'fore the first snowfall, I'll come back and build a hay mound opposite the trough. Then you'll be able to store all your grass inside."

"There you are!" Mother called out as she turned the corner of the cabin, wrapping her shawl around her shoulders. "I couldn't imagine where you'd all gone." Suddenly noticing the pole barn and Mr. Holbrook, she exclaimed, "Goodness glory! Whatever are you doing here, Mr. Holbrook? On the Lord's day, no less!"

Stopping in his tracks, Mr. Holbrook shifted the heavy wooden feedbox that had rested behind the cabin in his arms. "Forgive me ma'am, but if you'll give me a moment to set this down and fill it with dried grass, I'll be happy to explain and be on my way."

Mr. Holbrook disappeared into the pole barn, and Caroline quickly rushed to his defense. "He's been working here all morning, Mother," she said. "He told us he had to make a pole barn for Addie today because there was no other day he could do it, what with him working for Mr. Kellogg and all."

"And we didn't mind helping Mr. Holbrook one bit," Martha added.

"We collected all the grass he's putting in the feed box now," Eliza said. "Thomas is still jumping in the grass that's left over."

"I see," Mother said. "Henry and Joseph? You helped with the building?"

"I *told* him you didn't want us working on a Sunday," Henry exclaimed. "But he wouldn't listen to one word I said!"

"The shelter had to be built, ma'am," Mr. Holbrook said as he walked up behind Henry. "The children were a mighty help. I'd set more store by them than any of Kellogg's workers without thinking twice."

"Thank you for your kind words, Mr. Holbrook," Mother said, "and for spending your day of rest building Addie's barn. Now, if it's all the same to you, the rest of these fine workers look cold and hungry. And their dinner is getting colder with every minute we stand here. Inside now, children," Mother instructed. "Wash up quickly and get to the table."

"Thank you for understanding, and good day to you, ma'am," Mr. Holbrook said as he collected his tools. "I'll be seeing you 'fore first light."

Caroline didn't dare speak or look at Mother. But as she turned to walk to the house, she hoped that Mother would ask Mr. Holbrook to stay for dinner. He didn't smile much, but Caroline liked him.

As if she could hear Caroline's thoughts, Mother said, "You're welcome to join us, sir, if your family isn't expecting you. We've nothing fancy. But the stew's hot and hearty."

"If it's not a bother, I'd be much obliged," Mr. Holbrook answered without hesitation. "All the family I've got is back east. There's not a body in these parts expecting me for dinner."

Caroline looked from Martha to Eliza, grinning happily. Martha nodded, her eyes sparkling with excitement. Eliza simply looked cold and hungry. Together they rushed into the house.

Once inside, Mother spooned the stew into each bowl around the table. Joseph tossed another oak log on the fire and jabbed at it with an iron poker, releasing a flurry of sputtering sparks from the glowing logs below. The dimly lit room became bright and cheerful as flames leaped about the dry log. "There," Joseph said. "We'll be able to see much better now."

"Come spring, I'll have saved enough for windowpanes," Mother said confidently as she tucked Thomas's napkin into his collar and spread it over his shirt. "We've only three windows to buy for, and I'll not spend one more spring in a house with covered windows."

"For most of my growing years, I lived in a cabin that had hides on the windows," Mr. Holbrook said. "I spent every minute I could outside those dark four walls, and vowed that when I built my first dwelling, I wouldn't move in until all the windows had real glass panes."

"Have you built your home in Concord, Mr. Holbrook?" Mother asked.

"No, ma'am," Mr. Holbrook answered. "For another year or so I'll work for Kellogg; then I'll use my pay to buy me some land in these parts."

"I see," Mother replied, lifting a spoonful of stew to her lips.

Dappled in firelight, the cozy room was quiet for a moment as everyone dug hungrily into their tin bowls. Even though she knew it was bad manners, Caroline couldn't help watching Mr. Holbrook sip the steaming, chunky broth from his spoon, then wipe his furry beard with his napkin after each mouthful. She wondered how often he must trim such a beard, in order to keep it so neat and straight. Once his eyes caught hers across the table, and Caroline immediately began studying her bowl of stew.

"Do you have children?" Henry blurted out after a gulp of milk.

"Not a one," Mr. Holbrook said, before Mother could chastise Henry for asking such an impertinent question. "I've been alone in this world for years now. I expect I'll stay that way."

Her head still bowed, Caroline peeked up at the expressionless face of the man in front of her. She'd never before known anybody so serious. For two months this man had visited their home almost every day, but she had never seen him laugh at one of his co-worker's pranks, or tell his own jokes or tales. Mr. Holbrook wasn't lively or funny or charming like Mr. Ben, Uncle Elisha, or her own beloved father had been. But he was kind and gentle, and Caroline couldn't help but wish he weren't so alone.

Mr. Holbrook took his leave soon after dinner. "Thank you for your kindness yet again, ma'am," he told Mother. "And the children, too. They were fine helpers this morn. I'll be off 'fore candlelight, soon as I cut and split the same amount of wood I used for the pole barn."

"It isn't necessary to replace the timber," Mother protested. "We needed the shelter for the cow, and are most thankful for your help in building it."

"I told the boy I'd cut the wood so it'd weather through the winter for your real barn," Mr. Holbrook explained. "I intend to keep my word, Mrs. Quiner. Good day."

"Thank you, then," Mother said, closing the door behind him.

Sinking a dirty plate into the dishwater, Caroline looked up as Mother crossed to the stove. "What an odd man," Mother murmured.

"But nice," Caroline said.

"I think he should talk more," Martha declared.

"I think he has a funny beard," Eliza said.

"He certainly is helpful," Mother said, and set the pot of stew on the back of the stove where it would remain until supper.

Christmas Surprises

L ayers of ice and snow glazed the trees in the forest, icicles dangling from their crooked limbs like glittering baubles. But for the whirring rush of wintry gusts and the wails of a lonely wolf, the world was hushed. Day blended into day.

Late one evening, Mother sat down wearily on the high-backed settle beside Eliza and examined her sampler. "The satin stitches should be smoother there," she said, pointing to a row of uneven loops. "Same as you stitched them over here."

"These are my tired stitches," Eliza explained. "They're never as good as the others."

"Tired stitches?"

"The ones I stitch after we feed the workers," Eliza said matter-of-factly. "I'm more sleepy when I stitch them, so they're not as good. My Sunday stitches are best of all, because they're always my rested stitches."

"I see." Mother nodded. "Well, beginning tomorrow, you'll have three whole days to stitch your rested stitches. Maybe you'll even finish your sampler."

Joseph shaved a slice of wood off the kindling in his hand. It flipped through the air and landed on the pile of curly white shavings at his feet. "Mr. Kellogg's men aren't coming tomorrow?" he asked.

"Dear me!" Mother exclaimed. "Didn't I tell you?"

"No!" several voices rang out.

"Before Mr. Holbrook left this evening, he said that he and the other men will not be working for the next three days." Sighing happily, Mother continued, "I'd been wondering for weeks whether to expect seven or twelve for Christmas dinner. It's high time I learned Mr. Kellogg's plans, seeing how Christmas is but two days from now."

Caroline looked up from the gray yarn she was winding. "Two days until Christmas?" she asked. It didn't seem possible that so wonderful a day could come so unexpectedly. Caroline and her brothers and sisters had been so busy helping Mother care for Mr. Kellogg's men, they didn't have time to think about anything besides the next day's meals. But now, images of Christmas feasts and candies, presents and visitors crowded Caroline's thoughts. "Will Uncle Elisha come visit? Will he bring Grandma?" she asked.

"Maybe Mr. Ben and Charlie can come, too!" Martha exclaimed as she folded the wool sock she was mending and set it in her lap. "He always brings us plum pudding from Mrs. Carpenter on Christmas Eve."

"The Carpenters are spending Christmas with Mrs. Carpenter's family in Waukesha," Mother said. "And Uncle Elisha sent a letter saying that he is working feverishly on stories about Zachary Taylor's upcoming presidency. I'm afraid we won't see any of them until spring, children."

Kneeling in front of the hearth, Thomas tipped his wooden soldier upside down and dove him headfirst into the floorboards. "No pudding *and* no visitors for Christmas," he said, sulking.

"I'll miss them too, Thomas," Mother replied. "I should have started the fruit soaking for the plum pudding weeks ago, but I never gave it a thought. As it is, I've hardly had a free moment to plan anything for Christmas, so we'll have a simple, quiet day. I, for one, couldn't be more pleased that the seven of us will celebrate on our own!"

"Santeclaus will bring surprises, Mother," Caroline said with certainty. Just last Christmas, Uncle Elisha had told them about the jolly plump bearded fellow who carried an enormous sack of presents over his shoulder and put gifts in the stockings that children hung from their mantel on Christmas Eve.

Last year, Santeclaus had filled Caroline's stocking with five colorful Indian beads, a new scarf, and two pink wintergreen candies.

"I've never met this Mr. Santeclaus," Mother said, "so I've no way of knowing whether he intends to visit or not, Caroline. However, you should each hang a stocking from the mantel tomorrow night. Just in case."

On Christmas Eve morning, the sun rose in a silvery blue sky. The awakening winter world sparkled beneath it. Caroline and Eliza had just begun clearing the breakfast plates and cups from the table when there was a loud rapping at the door.

"It can't be Kellogg's men," Mother said, her voice rising in alarm. "I don't have any food prepared for them!" Straightening her apron, she smoothed her hair and walked across the cabin. Another knock clattered against the door as Mother pulled it open.

Caroline held her breath, squinting at the sudden glare from the open doorway, where she could see the outline of a tall figure.

"Morning, Mrs. Quiner," a man's deep voice greeted Mother. "I hope I'm not intruding at so early an hour."

"Why, Mr. Kellogg!" Mother couldn't keep the surprise from her tone. "We've only just finished breakfast. Please, come in."

"Only for a moment, if I may," Mr. Kellogg said. Stomping the crusty snow and ice from his boots, Mr. Kellogg stepped into the house and pushed the door shut behind him. The cabin grew dim and cozy once again.

"Might you care for a cup of coffee? Or tea?" Mother asked.

"No thank you," Mr. Kellogg declined. "Morning to you, young ladies," he greeted Caroline and her sisters. "Happy Christmas Eve."

"Happy Christmas Eve, sir," Caroline, Martha, and Eliza answered, smiling shyly.

Mr. Kellogg looked as imposing as ever in the small room. The bowl-rimmed hat nesting on the waves of his dark hair nearly touched the rafters. The smooth leather cloak covering him from shoulders to boots blocked the doorway altogether. In one gloved hand he carried a large sack, in the other a small pouch. Caroline wondered what was hiding inside.

"How is Mrs. Kellogg?" Mother asked.

"Every day she feels stronger," Mr. Kellogg replied, lifting his hat off his head. "My hope is that come spring, she'll be up and about as she used to be."

"We will hope as well," Mother promised.

"Thank you, Mrs. Quiner, for your good wishes, and for all your help these past months," Mr. Kellogg said. "Weren't for you, I'd have hung up my fiddle last fall and waited till spring to have my men begin clearing the land. As is, they'll be finished soon after the sap starts flowing, and I'll have forty acres ready for planting come May. I'm most appreciative, ma'am," he said, smiling warmly as he handed Mother the bundles.

"What is this?" Mother inquired, without looking into the sacks. Bursting with wonder, Caroline could hardly keep herself from running across the room to tear them open.

"I thought I'd bring you some food for the Christmas meal you'll be preparing, and thank you in person. The turkey was bagged last night, and the oysters arrived on ice from the Chesapeake Bay just yesterday. You should prepare them soon as possible or smoke them to keep them from spoiling. And don't forget to use the oyster crackers at the bottom of the bag. There's none tastier."

Looking incredulously from the sacks back to Mr. Kellogg, Mother said evenly, "Then you do expect me to cook Christmas dinner for your men, after all."

"Not by a jugful!" Mr. Kellogg corrected her, with a hearty laugh. "The bird and the oysters are for you and the children, Mrs. Quiner. I hope you'll enjoy every bite!"

"But this is far too much for us!" Mother exclaimed breathlessly, her face lighting up with delight. "And oysters, too. Why, we could make oyster soup, and stuff the turkey with oyster stuffing. Such a treat! Thank you, Mr. Kellogg."

"Thank you, Mr. Kellogg!" the girls echoed.

"Happy Christmas," Mr. Kellogg said, with a smile and a wink at Caroline.

Mother told her neighbor, "Perhaps if Mrs. Kellogg feels strong enough, you and your family would care to join us for dinner tomorrow. There will certainly be enough food."

"No thank you, Mrs. Quiner," Mr. Kellogg replied, bowing his head and placing his hat on it again. "For months now, you've cooked every meal for strangers. Christmas should be spent with your loved ones. Good day to all of you."

After Mr. Kellogg left, Mother rubbed her hands together merrily. "Oysters and turkey!" she exclaimed. "We will have a Christmas feast like we haven't had in years! And we'll begin this Christmas Eve with oyster soup."

Caroline couldn't remember any Christmas Eve that had smelled so good. After dinner, she and Martha peeled and cored a bowl of apples. Mother chopped and sprinkled the juicy white fruit with nutmeg and cinnamon and baked it into an apple crumb pie.

As the pie baked, Caroline mixed a dough

ball and set it in the dough box to rise. "May I help you braid the dough when it's ready?" she asked Mother.

"Of course."

"May I sprinkle the sugar and molasses mixture over the braid before we bake it?" Caroline persisted.

"You may just as well make the Christmas bread from start to finish, Caroline!" Mother laughed.

"Oh no," Caroline disagreed. "I've never braided bread dough before. And I don't know how to make your brown sugar topping, either."

"Then we shall do it together," Mother said. "But first, I need to get the oyster soup ready for supper."

Caroline watched as Mother drained the liquid from the frozen oysters and poured a portion of it into a small kettle of water that was heating on the cookstove. Crushing a handful of oyster crackers between her fingers, she sprinkled the crumbs over the hot liquid, added butter, and stirred. Once the steaming broth began to boil, Mother added half the oysters, milk, and cream to it, then seasoned the bubbly soup with pepper and nutmeg. The tangy, fishy steam curling out of the kettle of soup mingled with the sweet aroma of the baking pie. Caroline couldn't decide which smelled more delicious.

Savoring each spoonful of the tasty soup at supper, Caroline scraped every last oyster clump and bit of cream off the side of her bowl. Though she was warm and full inside when she finished, she held her bowl up for more soup the moment Mother began pouring seconds.

After supper, Caroline helped braid the Christmas bread and sprinkle the sweet, crumbly mixture on top. While Mother slid the bread into the dough box and secured the heavy door over it, she and her sisters ran to their room as Joseph and Henry followed Thomas up to the loft. Mother had just finished cleaning the turkey and rubbing it inside and out with salt and pepper when the children returned, ready for bed.

"May we stay up a while longer?" Martha asked.

"Just this once," Mother said. "But if you begin to feel chilled in your nightclothes, I expect you'll go to bed."

The cold winter air seeping into the cabin through cracks in the log walls was already sending shivers down Caroline's spine beneath her long flannel nightgown. But she didn't say a word. She wanted to stay up all night with Mother and help prepare the Christmas feast.

Leaning over the table, the girls watched Mother slice and cook the giblets and set them aside for gravy. Next, Mother chopped the rest of the oysters into little bits. Slowly, she heated the oysters in the frying pan with chopped onions, butter, and spices. Tossing handfuls of bread crumbs into the cooked mixture, she blended it into a lumpy, fragrant stuffing, then packed it into the turkey. "There," she said, smoothing butter on the bird's clammy skin. "It's all ready to begin roasting tomorrow morning. And now it's time to go to bed."

"We've brought our stockings," Martha said once Mother had finished washing and drying her hands.

"I brought one, too," Thomas chimed in. "But mine has a little hole where my big toe goes."

"Go find another stocking to hang, so the presents won't fall out if Santeclaus puts them in," Mother suggested.

The stockings were soon hanging from the mantel, longest to shortest. With one last look at the hearth, the girls dashed across the frosty floorboards, leaped under their quilt, and pulled it up to their chins, whispering and giggling excitedly as Mother kissed them good night.

Long into the night, Mother worked. On Christmas morning, she was standing at the cookstove before first light. Over the bell skirt of her gray wool dress, she wore a crisp white apron. A black shawl was draped over her shoulders, and a shiny silver net was wrapped around the hair knot she had rolled at the back of her head. As slices of salt pork sizzled on the cookstove, she whipped a bowlful of eggs until the yellow bubbles bubbled and climbed, one on top of the next, to the brim of the bowl.

"Happy Christmas, Mother," Caroline said, her eyes darting to the hearth where six stockings hung with bulges in their toes.

"He found us!" Henry cried, barreling down the rungs of the ladder that led from the loft. "Santeclaus was here!"

In a jumble of shouts and exclamations, the children bounded to the hearth one by one and pulled their stockings from the mantel. Caroline reached into her stocking and pulled out a pretty paper doll that had a long brown braid with a red ribbon drawn on it. The doll came with two print dresses and bows to match. Beneath the doll, she found two bright calico squares neatly stitched together.

"Santeclaus must think you're ready to begin sewing a quilt, Caroline," Mother said.

"And he must know I have a button collection, too," Caroline said happily, pulling a green button, a silvery button, and a china button out of the toe of her stocking. The china button had a tiny raised castle painted on it, with turrets rising straight off the tip of the smooth white circle.

Martha and Eliza also found buttons and paper dolls in their stockings. As they paused to examine each one, Mother asked, "Are your stockings empty now?"

Caroline turned her stocking upside down and shook it. "Yes, ma'am," she said.

"Then it's time for me to give you your other presents," Mother said, her eyes twinkling with excitement. "Girls first this morning."

Mother handed each of her daughters a small bundle that was neatly wrapped in scraps of red flannel. Carefully, Caroline pulled the soft material aside and discovered a small wooden box. A row of tiny hearts was carved across all four sides. A larger heart was carved in the center of the lid. The wood was dark and smooth, and Caroline lovingly ran her fingers across it, feeling each tiny carving. "It's so pretty!" she exclaimed.

"I've had these boxes for years, and now they belong to you," Mother told her daughters. "They could be used to keep most anything safe, but I expect you'll use them for all the buttons you've been collecting. Now for the boys—" she began, stopping mid sentence when she heard a rapping at the door.

"Sakes alive!" Mother exclaimed, getting up to open the door. "Who could be visiting this early on Christmas morning? It's not yet light out."

Mother pulled the door open, and Mr. Holbrook stepped out of the dusky light of daybreak into the dim cabin. "Morning, Mrs. Quiner," he said, puffing into one ruddy, wet hand that he had cupped over his mouth. A drift of powdery snow spilled onto the plank floor behind him, sparkling in the firelight like a mound of blinking stars. "Forgive the mess of snow I've drug in with me," he said, "and for my being a bit late, ma'am. I hope you haven't held breakfast for the other men."

Startled, Mother closed the door against the frigid morning air. "Why, Mr. Holbrook, it's

Christmas morning," she said. "All of the other workers are with their families today, as you yourself told us they would be."

"Christmas morning?" Mr. Holbrook said, his words hardly sounding like a question. "Forgive me, Mrs. Quiner. To acknowledge the corn, I plumb forgot. But that might explain why I found these packages leaning against your door," he said. Pulling his other hand out from behind his heavy pelt coat, he handed Mother three flat square packages that were wrapped in heavy brown paper and tied with twine.

"What are these?" Mother asked.

"I imagine they're Christmas presents for all of you. Careful, ma'am—they're awful heavy."

"Why, I . . ." Mother began. Accepting the packages from Mr. Holbrook, she carried them to the table and laid them down. "There are three," she said, "all the same size."

"One for the girls, one for the boys, and one for you, Mother," Caroline reasoned.

"Open them!" Martha said impatiently.

Gently pulling on the twine, Mother turned

the first package over and slowly unwrapped it.

"What is it?" Henry shouted as his sisters scrambled to the table to see for themselves.

Caroline looked down at the square of glass that was sitting snugly in the brown paper. She had never seen such a large piece of glass wrapped up like that before. The only other plates of glass she'd ever seen that were so large and thick had been tucked securely in the window frames of their house in Brook-field. "It's a windowpane, I think," Caroline said uncertainly.

"And there are two more!" Eliza exclaimed gleefully. "One for every window in our house."

"I bet Santeclaus left them by the door," Martha decided. "He couldn't fit them inside our stockings."

Mother looked at Mr. Holbrook.

"I'm sorry again for barging in like this, on a holiday and all," Mr. Holbrook said abruptly. "If indeed those are windowpanes, ma'am, I'll be happy to come by and fit them in the window frames the first warm day we get. It may be a Sabbaday, though. I'll give you fair warning."

"Thank you, Mr. Holbrook," Mother said, her voice shaky, but her eyes steady on Mr. Holbrook's face. "We could never thank you enough for such a favor."

"My pleasure," Mr. Holbrook answered. "Merry Christmas, Mrs. Quiner, children." Before Mother even had a chance to respond, or ask their visitor to stay for breakfast, he left the cabin.

Caroline was too distracted to watch Mother hand out the boys' gifts, and barely noticed Joseph giving Mother two small butter molds he had carved himself. The flash of firelight reflecting on the square windowpanes that now leaned on the top shelf of the dish dresser kept catching her eye. Caroline knew that Santeclaus hadn't wrapped those glittering panes in brown paper and left them outside the door. She knew the man who had really left them wasn't plump or jolly at all; he was a man who had only a strip of a beard, but who was very, very kind.

A Pot of Coals

B eing careful not to tilt the bowl and spill any of the steaming broth, Caroline carried a fourth serving of jackrabbit stew to the table and held it in front of Mr. Burgg.

"I'm afeared this old gut won't hold one more bite of your vittles, little girl," the shaggy man said as he rubbed his round belly. "I'm gettin all puny-feelin' as is, I jist ate so much. Bring me some of that coffee, and a spoonful or two of 'lasses to pour in. The more it tastes like shortsweetenin', the better."

"Yes sir," Caroline said. She carried away the hot bowl, and then brought Mr. Burgg his coffee and molasses, watching in amazement as he stirred spoonful after spoonful of the brown syrup into his mug.

"That's ezactly what I keered for," Mr. Burgg said. Tilting his head back, he gulped the drink, then held the mug bottom side up until every last drop of the gummy syrup had oozed into his mouth. Mr. Burgg smacked his lips, clanged the mug down on the table, and stood up to leave. "You make sure and have another drank, jist the same as t'other, waitin' for me in the morning, little girl."

"I'll tell my mother," Caroline promised.

One by one, Mr. Kellogg's men thanked Mother for their supper and ducked out into the blistering cold.

"Storm's come up like a thunderbolt," one man cried out.

"If that don't cap the climax," Mr. Hirch complained. "The snow ought to have come long before supper. We coulda stayed hum all day."

"Get on home, 'fore you're stuck but good," Caroline heard Mr. Holbrook respond. "Sudden squall like this can cause considerable trouble for folks who lose their way in it."

Caroline peered through the door at the wintry white blur whipping about the clearing. She wanted to peel back the hides covering the window frames and watch the storm but knew it was not possible. Ever since Christmas morning, when they had received the plates of glass, Caroline had waited for a warm day when Mr. Holbrook could put in the new panes. She was desperate to see sunlight brightening the cabin instead of the smoky kerosene lamps, and she missed seeing the stars flicker in the night sky. But mostly she missed the frosted patterns that had decorated the windowpanes of her house in Brookfield every winter morning, but never appeared on the leather hides. Until Mr. Holbrook fitted the new panes of glass, she could only listen to the wind shrieking outside the cabin and sneak a look out the door whenever someone entered or left the house.

On the long, weary days when she helped Mother cook and bake and clean all day, it was Caroline's only chance to see the outdoor world.

"It's February, no doubt." Mother grimaced, leaning against the door and shutting out the wind. Shivering, she hurried to the hearth and rubbed her hands together in front of the crackling flames.

Mr. Holbrook pulled his coat over his shoulders and headed for the door. "Another fine supper, Mrs. Quiner," he said. "Thank you kindly."

"I'll follow you out, Mr. Holbrook," Joseph said. "I'm going for an oak log." Wrapping a scarf knitted in gray and white squares around his neck, he reached for his coat.

"Don't expect us for breakfast, ma'am, if this storm gets any worse through the night," Mr. Holbrook said. "Long as it's near impossible to see, it's near impossible to clear any timber. I'll get word to you when Kellogg wants us working again. Evening, Mrs. Quiner, children."

"Thank you, Mr. Holbrook," Mother said gratefully. "We'll wait to hear from you. Be careful walking home."

Mr. Holbrook gazed down at his boots. "Will do, ma'am," he muttered. Yanking the door open, he walked out of the cabin, then stepped right back into the room. "What on earth?" he sputtered.

"What's wrong?" Mother asked, rushing to the door.

"What is it you want?" Mr. Holbrook called out.

"We need some hot coals, mister," a boy shouted above the wind.

Thinking she recognized the voice, Caroline quickly set down the dirty dishes Eliza had handed her and hurried up behind Mother. She peered past one side of Mother's skirt as the wind blew into her face. Two boys were huddled together in the doorway. Their snow-flecked hair flew wildly about; their flimsy, buttonless coats flapped in the wind. Shaking with cold, the boys had tucked their bare hands high up in their sleeves and were jumping in place, struggling to keep warm. Caroline's heart sank as she looked at Miles's and Wally's snow-streaked, red faces. "Those boys live by themselves in a shanty in our woods," she cried, tugging at Mother's skirt. "We have to help them, Mother."

"Come into the house," Mother coaxed the boys. "Hurry now!"

Miles stood his ground and pulled Wally toward him protectively. "We don't want nothing other than a few burning coals and a little iron pot to keep the coals alive till we get back to our diggings," he said. "I'll bring your pot back after sunup tomorrow."

"You're near frozen," Mother said, her voice rising. "Come inside and warm yourselves by the fire. Then tell us what's happened. We have some warm supper for you, if you'd like."

"It's too cold to keep the door open like this," Joseph added. "Come inside."

"I . . . I . . . I want t-to eat," Wally stammered, shaking with cold.

"Quiet, Wally," Miles said. "We have our own fixens at home. We just need a fire to cook them in." Turning his attention back to Mr. Holbrook and Mother, he asked proudly, "Are you going to give me those coals, or should we go asking at the next cabin?"

Caroline stepped up beside Mother and cried, "Miles, it's me, Caroline. You helped me find my way in that terrible storm, remember? It's only right that you let us help you and Wally now."

"We don't need nobody's help," Miles growled. "We need some burning coals, I told you. Seems not a body in this cabin wants to give them to us. Let's go, Wally. I know right where there's another homestead, not too far away."

Mr. Holbrook spoke up. "He won't make it another ten paces without falling over from cold and hunger. You his older brother, son?" he asked.

"It don't matter a hooter who I am," Miles said defensively, wiping the dripping snow off his face.

"Does to the boy," Mr. Holbrook said. "Seems to me he needs a warm place to stay and a good meal to eat before he walks one more step in this storm. If you were his big brother, which, ask me, I can't imagine you being, you'd do anything you could to take care of the boy, since he's too little to take care of himself."

"I take care of him better'n anybody!" Miles shouted.

Unruffled, Mr. Holbrook countered, "If you say so, I've no reason to believe any different. Wait right here, son. I don't want to see nobody freeze to death on account of something I did or didn't do. I'll close the door a minute and get you those coals."

Caroline watched Miles's sour expression turn to disbelief as Mr. Holbrook closed the door tightly, leaving the two boys standing outside in the screeching tempest.

"Whatever are you doing?" Mother demanded. "Those children could die in this storm!"

"That boy needs to decide to come into this cabin on his own, ma'am," Mr. Holbrook explained. "I'm simply giving him the time to do it. Now, where's there a pot that I can toss a few coals into?" he asked.

"You get the pot, Henry. I'll pull the coals," Joseph said. He grabbed the iron tongs that were hanging from the mantel, plucked out five glowing red coals from beneath the burning logs, and dropped them into the pot Henry was holding.

"Here are the coals you asked for, son," Mr. Holbrook's voice rang out as he wrenched the door open again. "Be sure and blow on them every second step from here to your house, or they're likely to snuff right out before you ever get to your shanty. Good luck to you both," he finished, and began to close the door.

"Wait just a minute, mister," Miles cried out. "I been thinking I could get back to our shanty quicker than greased lightning, were Wally able to stay here and warm up for a while. Maybe he could even eat a hot supper like the lady said, so when I get our fire going again and come back for him, he'll be strong enough to go with me. How's that sound, mister?"

"You his brother, son?" Mr. Holbrook asked loudly.

"Am that, mister," Miles answered.

"You what's left of his kin?"

"Am that, too."

"The boy needs you to stay with him right now then, I reckon," Mr. Holbrook said sensibly. "What if you lose your way in this storm, or fail to get your fire started again, for what reason only the Almighty knows? Me and your brother will come looking for you tomorrow or day after and find you lying cold as a wagon wheel somewheres in the forest. Maybe even in your own home. Who's the boy got to look after him then?"

"We'll stay just till Wally's warm again," Miles said finally. "But not one minute longer."

"Stay as long as you like," Mother said. She pulled both boys inside, and Mr. Holbrook shut the door against the storm one last time. The noise of the howling wind abruptly stopped.

Caroline watched for a moment as Mother pulled Wally's coat off and began rubbing his stiff red fingers and frozen cheeks to warm them. Then she walked over to Miles, who was standing sullenly by the door. Caroline felt a flash of anger at the boy. Why was he always so difficult?

"Taking help from others never hurt anybody, you know," Caroline said. "You shouldn't be so quick to do everything for yourself."

"Enough folks has tried to help us," Miles scowled. "Then they try to turn us into sons *they* want to have. Wally and me don't take to that kind of help."

"I never did either."

Caroline heard Mr. Holbrook's voice behind her, and she glanced over her shoulder to find him leaning against the log wall, his arms folded across his chest. Confused, she asked, "Never did what, Mr. Holbrook?"

"I never understood why some folks can't help a body just once and be satisfied that they did a good thing, Caroline," Mr. Holbrook explained. "There's some that want to help over and over again, and then decide what's best for somebody they don't even know. That's why Miles doesn't want help from anybody. Am I right, son?" he asked.

"It sure gets you in a fix," Miles agreed. Caroline was relieved to see the boy look more relaxed suddenly, and less like a cornered animal.

"I was in the same straits as you some years ago, Miles," Mr. Holbrook said, "but I had me a little sister to look after. Every time I let somebody feed us a meal, they ended up wanting to keep her and send me packing."

"Just like these folks do, I'll bet," Miles said, gesturing toward the table where Mother was holding a cup of warm tea to Wally's lips while Martha poured hot stew into a bowl in front of him. Both were murmuring softly to the little boy.

Mr. Holbrook shook his head and took hold of Miles's shoulders. Caroline had never heard him speak so gently "Only way you'll live, Miles, and keep your brother with you, is to figure out what folks you can trust. The Quiners, here, are folks you trust. Sit down now. Eat yourself some supper. If you decide once your belly's full that you can't ride out this storm here tonight, I'll go home with you and your brother and make certain your fire gets started. Then it's up to you to keep it from burning out again, and that's the last time you'll ever have to set eyes on me."

"I'll eat some supper," Miles said reluctantly. "But I won't promise nothing more."

"Ask your sister to serve up another bowl of stew please, Caroline," Mr. Holbrook said. Then he stood up and took off his coat.

Caroline pulled another chair to the table as Martha set down a bowl of jackrabbit stew and a cup of milk. Miles sat down without speaking or looking at either of them.

"He's not so grateful, is he?" Martha whispered to Caroline as she handed her the dirty dishes that had been left on the table.

Watching Miles gobble down the steaming stew and chunks of corn bread, Caroline answered, "I'm not so certain he has much to be grateful for."

Later, the Quiners finally sat down to supper, while Mr. Holbrook, Miles, and Wally quietly warmed themselves in front of the hearth. As she sipped the creamy milk from her mug, Caroline heard Miles ask, "What's your name, mister?"

"Holbrook. Frederick Holbrook," he replied. "And if I'm not mistaken, Henry and Joseph have some checkers here somewheres about. Maybe I can teach you boys how to play."

"Most everybody on earth knows how to play checkers," Miles scoffed.

"Then I won't have to feel one bit sorry when I beat you good," Mr. Holbrook answered.

Across the room, Caroline was astonished to see a smile cross Mr. Holbrook's face, answered by another from Miles.

Honey

"Where's Addie gone, Caroline?" Henry shouted.

Surprised, Caroline looked up so suddenly, she bumped her head against the wood of the henhouse she was cleaning. "Ouch," she cried, poking her head out of the crate. "Why couldn't you wait till I finished before you hollered at me like that?"

Henry looked down at his sister, concerned. "Addie's disappeared. I looked for her in the pole barn, behind the privy, outside the woodpile. She's nowhere to be found," he said gloomily.

"I milked her first thing this morning," Caroline said, rubbing the top of her head. "It wasn't all that long ago, so she can't have gone too—"

"I've looked around darn near this whole clearing," Henry interrupted gruffly. "I'll bet she's gone off into the forest."

"You best hope not, Henry," Caroline said. "It could take forever to find her."

"She's just days away from having her calf, I bet, and what's worse, we're supposed to give her back to Mr. Kellogg since Mother finished feeding all his workers for the last time last night," Henry muttered. "I better find Addie 'fore dinner, or Mother's going to give it to me good for losing her in the first place."

Inspecting the inside of the henhouse, Caroline decided it was clean enough. "If you help me get all the hens back inside, I'll come look for Addie with you."

Still pecking at the crushed corn that littered

the ground, the hens clucked and scattered as Henry shooed them back into their house. "Get in there, you nasty old rooster," he scolded the haughty bird. "I've more important things to do than spend the rest of the morning scrambling after you."

The rooster strutted his way into his house, squawking loudly at Henry's pestering. Caroline set the wooden bowl with the remaining bits of corn down beside the henhouse. "Let's go," she said.

"Wolf should come with us. He might find Addie before we do."

Loosening her shawl across her shoulders, Caroline waited while Henry whistled for Wolf. The air was warmer than it had been all spring, the sun brighter. But the thawing earth was still cold and muddy, and even though Caroline's worn boots pinched her toes and scraped the backs of her heels, she was happy not to have to search for Addie in her bare feet.

Wolf bounded across the clearing and pranced along as Caroline and Henry trekked into the woodlands. The forest was mottled with the soft blush of spring's early wild-flowers. Pink-petaled blossoms clustered on their reclining stems, and sprawling patches of droopy yellow lilies flowered between their portly leaves. Tightly wrapped buds clung to the branches of silvery green trees. Caroline walked along, breathing in the fresh spring air and spotting the perky squirrels, rabbits, and field mice that skittered about the forest.

"Addie's as brown as the trees, so she'll be hard to see from a distance," Henry said. He pushed a tangle of branches out of his way, holding them until Caroline passed. "Let's split up just far enough so we're in hollering distance. You take Wolf."

"The first one to see Addie hollers?"

"'Zactly."

On her own, Caroline moved ahead, step-ping over jutting vines and snapping dried branches as she called out for the cow and kept her brother's fair hair in sight. "Where are you, Addie?" she cried over and over. Then she stopped in her tracks. A fallen tree was lying in her path. Looking from one end of the trunk to the other, Caroline decided it would be faster to climb over the tree, rather than walk all the way around. Smoothing her dress carefully beneath her, she sat on the thick, bumpy trunk and swung her legs over the side.

Wolf barked loudly and began leaping about, his black snout high in the air.

"What is it, Wolf?" Caroline asked. "Do you see Addie?" Hastily, she scanned the forest, looking for Mr. Kellogg's cow. But Addie was nowhere in sight.

Vaulting over the trunk, Wolf landed softly on his paws, then soared into the air again, snapping his jaws and yelping. Caroline hopped off the tree and dashed to his side. "What's wrong?" she asked. "Why are you barking like that?"

Wolf stood his ground beside Caroline, barking and growling as she looked around to determine what was causing the fuss. When Wolf finally quieted down, Caroline heard a soft buzz. There, fluttering in a hazy column of sunlight above a knotted hole in the tree trunk, was a bee. Wolf began barking furiously once again.

"Quiet, Wolf," Caroline scolded. "It's just a little bee. You're supposed to be looking for a cow."

"Did you see her?" Henry called out as he raced across the forest, curls flying with every stump and fallen tree he hurdled. "Did Wolf find Addie?" he asked breathlessly.

"All he's found is a silly bee," Caroline replied. Glancing up at the sun that had already climbed high above the tips of the trees, she added, "Let's keep going, Henry, 'cause we can't look for Addie much longer. It must be close to dinnertime."

"Wait just a minute. Where did Wolf see that bee?"

"Right there," Caroline answered, pointing. "It was buzzing around that big hole in the tree."

"Stand still and be quiet. I want to see if any more bees fly by."

Caroline opened her mouth to protest, but

closed it again as another bee happened by and circled the round opening in the fallen trunk. Never losing sight of the bee, Henry immediately dropped to one knee beside Wolf and spoke to him in soothing tones. Wolf growled low in his throat but stopped barking. The bee remained suspended in the air, fluttering undisturbed.

Buzz. Buzzz. A second bee joined the first, and then a third. Soon a small circle of bees hovered and buzzed above the tree. "Today's a powerful lucky day, Caroline," Henry cried, slapping his knees and scrambling to his feet. "You've found us a honey tree!"

"A honey tree?" Caroline echoed, her voice full of wonder. "How do you know that?"

"All the bees buzzing into this one hole in the tree can't be nothing other," Henry promised. "Now we need to figure a way to mark it so it's clearly ours, and no one else will touch it come fall when all these bees are finished loading this old stump with their honey."

"Mark it how?"

"I need a rag, or something of the sort," Henry said, glancing up and down at his clothes, then at Caroline's. "Your shawl will work," he said. "Give it to me so I can tie it around the tree."

"But it's the only shawl I have!" Caroline exclaimed. "Mother will be furious with me if I leave it in the woods!"

"Mother will be so happy you've discovered a honey tree, she won't give a lick about your shawl."

"Well, what about Addie?" Caroline said sulkily, not wanting to give up her warm, soft garment.

"She won't be ready to be milked again till evening, so Mother doesn't have to know a thing about her," Henry said. "We'll have the whole afternoon to find Addie. As for your shawl, we can leave it on the tree just for now, and trade it for an old sock or something when we search for the cow after dinner. Nothing will happen to it between now and then, Caroline. Let's go."

Caroline handed Henry her shawl and

watched him carefully tuck it around the fallen tree. The April sunshine warmed her bare neck, and Caroline couldn't help feeling excited, even though they hadn't yet found Addie. "You're a good boy, Wolf," she whispered in the dog's pointy ear as she took one last look at the honey tree and imagined all the sweet honeycomb they'd scoop out of it come fall.

By the time they arrived back at the cabin, Caroline's side hurt from running so fast, and she was gasping for breath. But the moment Henry tossed the door open, she burst inside and cried, "Mother! We found a honey tree in the forest! Henry marked it so the honey will be all ours come harvesttime!"

As she took a deep breath, Caroline realized that Mother was not alone in the small room. Mr. Holbrook was seated at the table beside another man whom Caroline had never seen before. The man was dressed in black. His large, pocked face was covered with black beard stubble, and his graying hair was cropped close to his head. Caroline stared into the man's blue eyes, which were kind and piercing all at once, and she was certain that eyes like that would know that Addie had disappeared, no matter what wonderful news Caroline and Henry had to tell. Before Mother could say a word, Caroline stammered, "I'm sorry for interrupting, Mother. I just wanted to tell you about the honey tree. I didn't know you had folks visiting."

Mr. Holbrook quickly stood up from the table. "This is Mr. Speakes, Caroline," he introduced the man. "He's come to have dinner with us. Mr. Speakes, this is Caroline, the last of Mrs. Quiner's daughters."

"Happy to meet you, sir," Caroline said politely.

"And you," the man replied without standing.

"That's fine news about the honey tree," Mother said. "Now wash your hands and face, then go brush your hair. Dinner's near ready."

Caroline headed for the washstand, scrubbed her face and hands, then disappeared into her room to brush her hair. Eliza was seated on one corner of the straw tick. Martha was standing above her, dividing and tucking strands of her sister's silky hair into long gold braids.

"Who's that man with Mr. Holbrook?" Caroline whispered.

"He's the circuit rider," Martha answered. "Mr. Holbrook brought him along to meet Mother, and she's invited them both to stay for dinner."

Pulling the ribbon off the bottom of her braid, Caroline ran her fingers through her hair, loosened it, then brushed it with long strokes. "What's a circuit rider?" she asked.

"Joseph says he's a man who travels by horse from town to town, visiting folks who don't have a church to go to or a preacher nearby. He says a circuit rider once visited us in Brookfield 'fore they ever built the church, but I don't remember that. Now finish your braid, Caroline, so we can go back into the other room," Martha said. "You can go first."

"You're the oldest," Caroline countered as she tied her green ribbon around the bottom of her braid and swung the braid over her shoulder. "*You* go first."

"I'll go first," Eliza said, and she marched to the dinner table, her sisters following behind.

Once Mother had served the hot bean porridge and fried fish, the circuit rider bowed his head and began giving thanks in solemn tones. Before Caroline had a chance to reach for her spoon, he was already speaking about his travels and sharing news of the day.

"As you surely know, Mrs. Quiner," he began, "General Zachary Taylor's been elected the President of our United States."

"I am aware of that, sir," Mother said.

"A slaveholder, he," Mr. Speakes pointedly remarked. "Mind you, he's said to oppose the expansion of the despicable institution, but I say how's a man who has his own slaves supposed to make other men understand slavery is against the will of God Almighty?"

"You're an abolitionist, then, Mr. Speakes?" Mother asked.

"Preach it everywhere I can, ma'am," the circuit rider answered. "Every person's got certain rights, as I see it, no matter what color he is. Or if he happens to be a she, for that matter. We're all the same in the eyes of God Almighty. Remember that, children," he said, looking around the table. "Last town I visited, Mrs. Quiner, I met a man and his missus who traveled all the way to New York this July past to discuss the rights of ladies such as yourself. They say wagonloads of women showed up from all parts of the country. And plenty of menfolk were there, too."

Mother smiled. "In my early years in Boston, I frequented such meetings," she said. "These days, I'm too busy doing whatever work I can to keep my family fed."

"Mrs. Quiner's been working for Mr. Kellogg these past many months since his wife took ill," Mr. Holbrook explained to the circuit rider. "Now Mrs. Kellogg's back on her feet again, and all of Kellogg's laborers, myself included, ate our last supper here last night, with great regret. If you should hear of any other townsfolk needing such help during your stay here—"

"I'll be certain to tell you, Mrs. Quiner," Mr. Speakes promised. "Perhaps you might head out west, though," he suggested. "Rumor is gold's been discovered in California. Folks is getting plenty rich quick."

"'He that trusteth in his riches shall fall,'" Mother quoted. "Isn't that correct, Mr. Speakes?"

"Good Lord's words, they," Mr. Speakes agreed. "But were I another sort of man, I'd load my wagon and risk my hide to find me a tea caddy full of gold nuggets."

"I'd be grateful just to have the crop we plant this spring be fruitful," Mother said. "Would you care for more fish, Mr. Speakes?"

"We'll pray for that, ma'am," Mr. Speakes answered. "For the planting, I mean. As for the fish, I've spent so much of this meal flapping my lips, I've barely had a bite of this fine food." He studied his plate. "I love fried fish, though, and this appears to be mighty tasty. Please save an extra morsel for me, Mrs. Quiner."

"Tell more about the gold!" Thomas spoke

up as he lifted his plate for second helpings.

"Mind your manners, Thomas Quiner," Mother warned.

"Could we *please* hear more about the gold?" Henry pleaded.

"Your boys have got a thirst for adventure!" Mr. Speakes laughed merrily, his chin bouncing up and down as he gobbled a bite of fish.

In between bites, Mr. Speakes kept the Quiners entertained with stories of the gold rush. Fascinated, Caroline listened to his tales as she absentmindedly ate her dinner. She didn't understand many of the grand words the circuit rider used, but she knew that Mother would explain all of them to her, if only she remembered to ask.

After dinner, Mr. Speakes stood up slowly from the table and breathed a great sigh of satisfaction. "It's been a mighty fine afternoon for me," he said, snapping his black suspenders against his black shirt. "I wish I had time to whistle a few tunes on my harmonica, or read a favorite selection from the Good Book, but I'm due with my saddlebags at your neighbor Worthman's cabin 'fore supper. Sad fellow. His most productive cow dropped dead not a week ago, and he wants me to say a blessing over the rest of his herd 'fore I leave town."

"When will you be coming through again?" Mr. Holbrook inquired as he followed the preacher to the door.

"In two months' time I'll return to christen the infant that James Tobey and his missus are expecting. I'll marry a couple or two, and the Lord knows I'll have a grave to pray over," he added, lifting the heavy saddlebag he had propped against the door and swinging it over his shoulder. "If you're willing, Mrs. Quiner, you might take part in a camp meeting where you and your neighbors can worship and sup together. The Lord smiles down on such an event, no doubt about it."

"We'd love to attend," Mother agreed, her face brightening at the very idea.

"I'd be happy to escort you and the children, ma'am," Mr. Holbrook offered.

"Thank you, Frederick," Mother replied.

Bewildered, Caroline looked over at Martha, who shrugged her shoulders in confusion. Each day for months Mr. Holbrook had eaten his meals at their home, but Caroline couldn't remember Mother ever calling him by his first name.

"I'll count on seeing you in June, then," the preacher said. "Good day, and thank you, Mrs. Quiner. Your children are fine listeners." With a wave and a quick blessing, the circuit rider was gone.

"I'll see to Addie," Mr. Holbrook told Mother.

The room felt suddenly warm to Caroline. She had forgotten about Addie! Heart racing, she tugged at Henry's sleeve.

"What do you need with Addie?" Henry asked calmly, squeezing Caroline's hand behind his back.

"I want to make certain she's still in the pole barn," Mr. Holbrook answered.

"She was in the pole barn when Caroline milked her 'fore sun up. That right, Caroline?" Henry asked cautiously.

"Yes," Caroline replied honestly, but her

cheeks flushed. She wished she had told Mother that Addie was lost hours ago.

"I'm sure she was," Mr. Holbrook said. "But on my way here with the Reverend, I found Addie down by the riverbank chomping her way through a patch of clover. I had to coax her all the way back to the pole barn. We don't want to take any chances that she'll disappear into the woods again today, especially since she's about to give birth and is due back to Kellogg tonight."

"No sir," Henry agreed, flashing a grin of relief over his shoulder at Caroline. "We'll keep an eye on her until you leave." Caroline nodded vigorously.

"Be certain to tell us before you go," Mother said as she looked up at Mr. Holbrook and smiled warmly.

"Will do," Mr. Holbrook promised. Then he stepped away to look after Addie.

Martha and Eliza began cleaning the dinner dishes. Caroline swept the floor and told Mother and her sisters how she had stumbled upon the bees and their honey tree.

"Such luck, finding a honey tree so easily," Mother exclaimed. "Most folks have to spend a whole day following a bee to its home. I'd much prefer bumping into a honey tree the way you did, Caroline."

Mother seemed so happy, Caroline even confessed that she'd left her shawl behind in the forest to mark the tree. "Henry and I didn't have any other way to find the beehive when we went back for it," she quickly explained.

"Just get the shawl as soon as we've finished," Mother advised, not troubled at all.

The blazing ball of sunlight was already tipping downward into the forest's treetops when the girls dashed outside. Martha and Eliza headed for the river to make grass dolls, while Caroline ran to find Henry.

The boys were busily underbrushing a patch of forest that bordered the clearing behind the cabin. "If we can clear even this much more land before planting time, we'll double our yield," Joseph was saying as Caroline came upon them. "We'll have to work fast, since we have only a few weeks before we need to begin turning the soil and getting it ready for planting."

"Mr. Holbrook says he'll take down the tallest trees," Henry said. "I say we use all the help we can get!"

"Henry!" Caroline hollered. "I have to get my shawl, and you have to come along to show me where it is!"

Looking up from the thorny bush he was dragging across the ground, Henry called back, "Did Mother give you a rag to trade it with?"

"I forgot to ask," Caroline admitted, shaking her head.

"Well, go get one that's long and colorful," Henry instructed. "No sense in making a trip to the tree if we've nothing to mark it with."

Caroline ran back to the cabin. Just as she was about to turn the corner of the house, she heard Mr. Holbrook saying, "You've two months then to decide if my proposal suits you, Charlotte. The Reverend Speakes can surely accommodate us when he returns in June."

Caroline froze in her steps. She peeked

around the corner of the house. Mr. Holbrook and Mother were standing close together outside the front door.

"You'll know my decision as soon as I've made it," Mother said. "Good day, Frederick. Please visit again soon."

Mr. Holbrook hesitated, then asked, "You're certain you and the children will be able to make do without Kellogg's wages?"

"Mr. Kellogg has been more than generous," Mother said. "As long as we harvest a good crop, we'll have enough food to take us through the year, and provisions to spare. I may be able to get some sewing work, as well. It's a whole lot easier than feeding hungry laborers every day."

"Rest assured I'll help in whatever way I can," Mr. Holbrook vowed, "no matter what your decision, Charlotte. And please tell Caroline and Henry that I'd be happy to teach them how to raise their own bees next spring, if they'd like. Good afternoon."

Standing stiff as a tree trunk against the house, Caroline waited, not daring to breathe.

Listening for the cabin door to close, she watched Mr. Holbrook disappear into the woods. Thoughts and questions skipped about her mind as she tried to make sense of the conversation. But she couldn't.

Caroline gently pushed the cabin door open. Catching sight of Mother's peaceful face across the room, she suddenly realized she didn't need to make sense of anything at all. Twelve whole months had passed since the wagon loaded with all their belongings had first rolled across the little clearing full of stumps, and stopped abruptly outside the tiny dwelling. Now, the cabin, the clearing, and the budding woods beyond were the Quiners' home—the sparkling windowpanes; the rich, cleared soil; caring neighbors; and new friends like Mr. Holbrook. The hardest work Mother and the children had ever done was finally finished, and the smile that Caroline remembered on Mother's face years ago shone there once again.

"I've come to get a rag to mark the honey tree, Mother," Caroline said. "Henry says it should be extra long, if you have one."

"Look in my scrap bag by the sewing table," Mother said. "Everything I have is in there."

Caroline found a bright-red rag and thanked Mother. Running across the clearing with it, she glanced back at the little cabin. Everything I have is in there, she thought happily, and sped off into the warm April afternoon, the scrap of red calico fluttering in the air behind her.